The Last Cherry Blossom

The Last Cherry Blossom

KATHLEEN BURKINSHAW

Sky Pony Press
New York

Sky Pony Press books may be purchased in bulk at special discounts for sales promotion, corporate gifts, fund-raising, or educational purposes. Special editions can also be created to specifications. For details, contact the Special Sales Department, Sky Pony Press, 307 West 36th Street, 11th Floor, New York, NY 10018 or info@skyhorsepublishing.com.

Sky Pony® is a registered trademark of Skyhorse Publishing, Inc.®, a Delaware corporation.

Visit our website at www.skyponypress.com.

10 9 8 7 6 5 4 3 2 1

Library of Congress Cataloging-in-Publication Data is available on file.

Jacket design and illustration by Katy Betz

Print ISBN: 978-1-63450-693-9
Ebook ISBN: 978-1-63450-694-6

Printed in the United States of America

This book is dedicated with love to the memory of the Ishikawa family and to all who died under "that famous mushroom cloud." Most of all, it is dedicated to my mother—the strongest, bravest woman I have ever known. I am proud to be your daughter. I love you and miss you very much.

CHAPTER ONE

"IMPERIAL JAPANESE ARMY CONTINUES
SUCCESSFUL ATTACKS AGAINST CHINA."

Showa 19 August 24, Thursday Edition

"Get under your desks—now!" Yakamura-sensei shouted above the lonesome wail of the air raid siren. The teacher's voice did not waver as she barked this command. Her lips were pursed in a thin line, yet her hand had a slight tremor as she pointed toward the floor.

My stomach lurched. I could hear my heart beating in my temples, my legs wobbled as if made of cooked ramen. I was torn between wanting Sensei to review and grade my koseki project and wanting to run for cover. I froze.

"That means you, too." Yakamura-sensei nudged my elbow to move me away from her desk and back to my own.

The familiar hum of the B-sans—what we called the American B-29s that flew overhead—thundered in my ears.

The engines were so loud that the floor vibrated under my feet. I covered my ears and scurried beneath my desk. I pulled my knees up to my chin. I stretched my uniform skirt down over my ankles and wrapped my arms around my knees, clasping my hands together.

The air raid sirens blared at least twice a day now. You would think I would have been used to them, but my pulse still raced whenever the eerie siren sounded, followed by the rumbling of the B-sans. And, every time, I worried. *Will we actually get bombed? What if the school collapses? Will this desk actually protect me? Is my papa safe? How will I find him if a bomb hits us? Is Machiko as scared as I am, in her classroom down the hall? Why do I always have to go to the bathroom when I am nervous?*

I heard the scraping sound of a desk moving. I looked up to see one of my classmates rocking her body back and forth. Next to her I spotted one boy reading *Shou-chan* manga. *How can he be so calm at a time like this?*

I rested my chin on my knees and tried to think about something else. I blew away the stray hairs that fell out of my braid. My hair never stayed neatly braided like the other girls' in my class. My stomach growled. *I wonder what type of fish our maid Fumi-san will be serving for dinner tonight. I really hope that I can show my koseki project to Yakamura-sensei when this air raid warning ends. I want to impress her with what I learned about my samurai ancestors.*

The all-clear siren soon interrupted my thoughts. The

class let out a simultaneous sigh of relief. The cramp in my fingers made it difficult to unclasp my hands. When I did, I noticed my white knuckles had nail marks dug into them. One by one, we emerged from the shelter of our desks. I bumped my head on the desk as I moved. "Ouch!"

The most annoying twelve-year-old in my seventh grade class, Taro-kun, heard me. He shook his head and sang his all too familiar rhyme, "Yuriko dojikko." He laughed. *Did he really think I was unaware of how clumsy I am?*

Yakamura-sensei announced that we would all need to go home, which we knew already—it was also a part of the daily air raid routine.

As the rest of my classmates gathered their books and bags, I went straight to my teacher's desk and pleaded, "Sensei, may I please have my grade on the koseki project?" For a change, I had worked really hard on this week's homework assignment. I wanted to hear what she thought of my ancestors from the Sugawara clan who fought in the famous Battle of Sekigahara in 1600. Papa, Mama, and I were the last branch of the family tree. I had also added that my papa worked his way up to owning his own newspaper in Hiroshima after being raised on a corn farm. If Sensei praised my project while my classmates were still in the room, and if they overheard that, maybe they'd find me interesting enough to be their friend.

Sensei pulled out my koseki project from a folder on her desk. She nodded as she began reading about each ancestor. But then she raised her eyebrows and slowly moved her head from side to side. She bit her lower lip and said slowly, "That is not right."

My smile disappeared. This was not the response I had expected. I almost blurted out the "arigato" I had planned, but instead, I stared at her. My cheeks were burning and I knew they were as red as the sun on Japan's flag. My fists tapped against the side of my legs.

The room was unbearably silent. The students who had not yet left the classroom had their eyes trained on me. I knew they were listening and that this was my chance to impress them, so I cleared my throat a few times, hoping it would help push my words out.

"What do you mean?" My voice made a funny squeaking sound on the last word. At that moment I wished I had flown away with the B-sans.

My teacher stared at me. She gave me a quick, weak smile and then stood abruptly. "I am sorry. This is a wonderful project. Please excuse me, I am late for a meeting and must leave right away." She hurried out the door. I was stunned at her response. The rest of my classmates who had witnessed the scene quickly filed out of the room.

I went to my desk to gather my things so I could run after Sensei. But as I lifted the books from my desk, my hands fumbled and all the books fell to the floor. *Yuriko dojikko* echoed in my head. I picked them up. By the time I left the room, my teacher was nowhere to be found so all I could do was head home.

4

On my walk, I kept repeating Sensei's words to myself: "That is not right. That is not right." The more I thought about it, the faster I walked, until I found my legs running toward home.

I went around to the side entrance of my house, sliding the shoji door open and shut with the stealth of a ninja. I braced myself against the door, trying to catch my breath. When I could finally breathe normally, I kicked off my shoes, sank into the western-style wicker chair, and sighed. The study was my favorite room in the house. It was where I went to be by myself. All along the walls were mahogany bookcases filled with books whose characters were my first friends. It didn't matter if the books were children's adventure stories, history books about our samurai ancestors, or reference texts for my papa's newspaper articles—I loved reading them all. Sitting in there with a book on my lap, I was able to forget about being lonely and about the war.

But today I couldn't concentrate on the words and sat fidgeting in my chair, my brain racing. My foot tapped the floor uncontrollably.

In my head, I still heard my teacher reviewing my koseki project. Her four words about the family tree—*That is not right*—played over and over in my head like the *drip, drip, drip* of water hitting pebbles in our fountain. What wasn't right about the tree? There had been whispers about my parents behind my back—I knew that—but I never let it bother me as Papa had always said that people gossiped about our family because of our wealth and the fact that he ran his own newspaper. Whenever I questioned him about it, he told me that we were expected to be above gossip and to ignore any rumors. I never gave it a second thought, until now.

But this was the first time someone had said something directly to me. *Why did Sensei leave so quickly? Why did she change her answer? Why did she nod in agreement and then suddenly say what she said?*

"Joya, young lady, are you here?" my papa's booming voice called out. He slid the door open and I jumped out of my chair into his outstretched arms.

"Welcome home, Papa!"

Even when I was only as tall as his knees against his six-foot frame, Papa would easily swoop down, pick me up, and hug me close. Even though he could no longer pick me up, he still held me tight. I breathed in the cologne he wore all the way from the top of his balding head down to his feet. I never felt safer than when I was in his arms.

"Joya, did you have a good day at school?" he asked me.

"It was a strange day."

"Oh? Well, we will discuss that after my bath." He released his bear hug and walked toward the stairway, turned back to face me, saying, "Yuriko, I want to remind you to finish your homework before dinner on Sunday. We will be having a guest."

"Who is coming for dinner?"

"Sumiyo-san."

I wracked my brain trying to remember who she was. "Is she the lady who brought us meals and shopped for us after . . . after Mama died?" My voice hitched, and I tried to swallow the lump in my throat.

Papa walked back to me and hugged me again. "Yes." He cleared his throat. "She has returned to Hiroshima. We will be welcoming her back as well as thanking her for her kindness during that time." He broke the hug and started to walk upstairs again.

"Oh, Papa, can I talk to you about what happened at school before you take your bath? It was so—"

Fumi-san interrupted me. "Excuse me, Ishikawa-san, but the copy department called. They need you back at the office."

"I see." Papa turned to me and said, "This can wait until tomorrow morning at breakfast, neh?"

I nodded. "Yes, Papa."

He kissed my forehead and went out the kitchen door.

I headed upstairs to start on my homework. When I got to my room, I found my books scattered all over the floor. And this time, I hadn't left them that way. In the corner, all my desk drawers were opened. I knew exactly who was responsible. My five-year-old cousin loved to mess up my room. Sometimes, he would hide my stuff. He was a menace. As I began putting my books back on their shelves, I muttered to myself, "You moved into my home and messed up everything. I don't—"

I picked up my copy of *Urashima Taro*, about the famous

7

Japanese folk legend. It was my very favorite of all the books I owned. I had read it over and over again since I was very young. But now I saw that the cover was torn! I marched out of my room and yelled, "Genjiiiiii! Genji, you are in big trouble this time!"

CHAPTER TWO

*"WE WILL NEVER CEASE FIRE UNTIL OUR
ENEMY CEASES TO BE."*

Showa 19 August 25, Friday edition

I rolled over to pull the blanket up to my chin. My eyelids
fluttered open as I yawned. It was still dark outside, so I figured I had more time to sleep, but our neighbor's rooster was
telling me otherwise. I needed to finish the homework that I
should have done before bed instead of mending the cover of
Urashima Taro. It really bothered me that Genji didn't even
have to help me clean up *his* mess. Aunt Kimiko made him
apologize, but as soon as she left the room he stuck his tongue
out at me and ran after her.

I could think of reasons to be angry at Genji all morning,
but I still had homework to do. I crawled off my futon and
grabbed my schoolbag from the bottom of my closet where I
had thrown it last night. I turned on my desk lamp, my eyes

squinting against the harsh artificial light.

The homework assignment was to write in our journal about a favorite childhood memory. As I sat down to begin the entry, I became five years old again:

"Do it again, Papa! Please, one more time." Papa chuckled and then cupped his hands over his mouth and hooted like an owl. It made me laugh to hear such a tall, serious man make such a joyful, high-pitched sound. That was how we spent our summer nights out on the veranda. The gentle breeze felt good after a hot bath. We both sat on the rattan sofa with our feet up on the coffee table. Papa told stories of our samurai ancestors, acting out battle scenes by changing his voice for each character.

He would say, "We can laugh, little one, as long as you remember that you should have pride because of your ancestry. No one can ever take that from you. Family and honor are very important. You must never forget that, neh?"

To break the seriousness, he again made the call to the owls. Before I gave him a hug and kiss good night, I would gently rub some ointment onto his neck. His arthritis would always be worse at the end of the day. The medicine had such an awful smell, and I hated that it was so sticky and hard to wash off my hands. But I gladly used it for Papa because I knew it made him feel better.

Loud knocking on my door brought me back to the present. My Aunt Kimiko slid the door open, not even bothering to wait for me to say, "Come in."

"Yuriko-chan, you must eat breakfast now. You are late—

not like that is a surprise." She shook her head when she saw my homework notebook open.

"I am late because I had to repair the book that Genji ruined."

"Yuriko-chan, I made him apologize. Besides, you did not have to fix the book last night."

"You could have made him help me clean it up, too."

"It is not as if you normally keep your room pristine. When I was your age, I was responsible for keeping my room neat and tidy. And you can't blame everything on Genji-chan. He is only five years old." Aunt Kimiko turned and left the room.

I wanted to scream. Aunt Kimiko only spoke to me when she wanted to criticize or order me around. And it was always with an edge in her voice. She saved her softer, nicer voice for the times when she spoke to me in front of Papa. And for Genji, she always had an excuse: "Genji is too young. Genji is a boy."

I returned to my journal, completing the last sentence. I held my pencil so tightly and pressed so hard that the tip broke just as I finished writing the last word. I sighed. As I put another pencil into my bag, my stomach growled. The sweet smell of kasutera wafted into my room. I zipped up my bag and went downstairs to the dining room.

I looked around the table and realized I had a rare moment alone with Papa. I could finally ask him about my koseki project.

"Papa, Yakamura-sensei said something to me in class

that I did not understand yesterday." I took a sip of my miso soup and grimaced at its bitter, salty taste.

"Oh?"

"When I handed in my family tree project, the teacher said that something was not right about it."

Papa looked at me with wide eyes, his brow furrowing. "What koseki project, Yuriko-chan?"

I knew something was odd because he called me by my name and not Joya, his nickname for me, so I said, "I did not mention it while I was working on it because I knew the answers. And I was so proud of our samurai heritage that I wanted to surprise you with it. But she confused me with her comment."

"Hmpf," he huffed, then pushed back his chair and headed into his study. Before I could say anything, he dialed the phone and asked for Yakamura-sensei. Then he slid the door shut and I couldn't hear the rest of the call.

"Yuriko-chan, you will be late! Go put on your school uniform," my aunt commanded.

"But I—"

"Go!"

I sighed, turned, and slouched up the stairs, stomping on each one. On any other day I would have argued with Aunt Kimiko, but I did not want to interrupt Papa's phone call with our shouting.

Back in my room, on the bottom of my closet floor, was my starched uniform balled into a heap. The white sailor shirt with the blue scarf made me look like I was five years old. And the pleated skirt was itchy. But I put them on nonetheless. In a feeble attempt to get out the wrinkles, I pressed my hands down the length of my skirt, then I gathered my books and ran down the stairs to meet Papa at the front door.

As I passed the hall window, I looked out, hoping to see a funeral procession. I hadn't seen one yet, but according to Papa's superstition, if a funeral passed by before he left the house, he would stay home. I held out hope that it meant I could stay home, too.

I reached the entryway and put on my shoes as Aunt Kimiko approached me. "Your papa said he will be going in later this morning. His driver will take you to school today."

The day was not off to a good start. Not only was Papa not staying home but he wasn't going to join me on the way to school. I slumped into the car and the chauffeur and I drove in silence. I kept thinking about what Papa said to the sensei on the phone and what that would mean for me in class today.

CHAPTER THREE

"OUR IMPERIAL ANCESTORS HAVE FOUNDED
OUR EMPIRE ON A BASIS BROAD
AND EVERLASTING."

From the Imperial Rescript read at schools

When I got to school, I was surprised to see that the sensei was not in our class and the principal was acting as our substitute teacher for the day. Perhaps Yakamura-sensei was ill. But I couldn't help but wonder if her absence had anything to do with Papa's phone call this morning.

Like every morning, we went outside for our yard exercises and then sang our national anthem, "Kimigayo," also known as "Long Live the Emperor." During the singing, a picture of the Emperor was paraded past us and I bowed with the other students so that we would not look upon his sacred image. The principal then made announcements about the victory in the Pacific and reiterated our need to be loyal citizens during the Great East Asian war.

For my age group, our war involvement meant learning to handle bamboo spears that the boys in our class made for our gym class. The spears were made of bamboo because metal had become hard to find.

I took my spear in my right hand. I closed one eye and aimed at the target on a scarecrow a few yards away. Time and time again I tried but was unable to hit the target. But, I did almost stab the person next to me once.

I came to the conclusion that for me to wield a bamboo spear with some accuracy into a target *and* with force was like expecting a dog to learn a waltz.

At first, the team captains had wanted me on their teams because of my family's samurai history. However, after the first race I ran as part of a team, that all changed. I had wanted to run my very best to make Papa proud of me. I pushed myself to run as fast as I could, but I was still the last one to cross the finish line. When I looked up, Papa was beaming me a smile. He told me, "Joya, I am very proud of you. Remember that many Japanese fables are about having patience when we cannot get to something fast enough. It is the one who learns the art of patience that is the true winner."

But the team captains didn't share this belief.

And patience was not helping me spear this scarecrow, either. The gym teacher lost *his* patience and yelled, "Yuriko-san, scream louder and hit harder!"

"Yuriko-chan, I hope you never see the enemy, because

we will be doomed!" laughed Taro-kun, as he made a gesture of his head being chopped off. Taro-kun enjoyed picking on me. When we were nine years old, he followed me home just to throw a rat snake at me. He knew I was afraid of snakes. The snake hit my heel and I was so scared that I was sick for a week with a nervous stomach and headache.

So I took great pleasure in nonchalantly putting my bamboo spear out just enough so that he tripped on it as he walked by.

After the pathetic bamboo spear exercise, the morning flew by. Following lunch, I spent sewing class daydreaming of what it would be like if I were the bamboo spear champion. The last part of the day was devoted to working on our journal project. The subject today was friendship and we were supposed to write about a special memory from our childhood. I did not have much trouble with this assignment and began to write:

When I was younger, Papa insisted that I had to stay within our gated yard. I didn't play with the other children in our neighborhood. He told me that he worried someone might kidnap me for a ransom and he couldn't bear anything happening to me. So, our maid, Fumi-san, would play with me in the backyard and watch me swim in our koi pond. I loved splashing around and pretending to be the magical turtle from Urashima Taro, except for when the koi fish would nibble on my belly. The pond could be seen by anyone walking on the side street.

One morning, as I was trying to swim away from the koi,

I sensed that someone was looking at me. I turned. A man dressed in a business suit stood on the other side of our iron gate. He bowed, tipped his hat, and said, "Ohayo, little girl."

"Good morning," I said as I waved to him. He waved back and continued on his way.

"Fumi-san, do you know who he is?" I asked the maid.

"Hmm . . . no. Maybe he is new to the neighborhood."

"I think he is sad, Fumi-san. His eyes frown even when his mouth smiles."

"Yuriko-chan, you are so silly." Fumi-san shook her head and laughed.

The next morning, I could not wait to go out to the pond. I wanted to see if the new neighbor would walk by again. After a few minutes of splashing at the fish, I saw the man in the suit. I rushed to greet him. "Ohayo gozaimasu."

Again, he tipped his hat as he replied, "Good morning, little girl."

Once he left, I turned to Fumi-san and said, "I still think he looks sad, don't you?"

"Yuriko-chan, I do not know what you are talking about."

"Maybe next time I will ask him if he is sad."

"No, Yuriko-chan, it is rude to ask that. It is none of your business. Do you understand?"

"Yes, Fumi-san, I understand."

Every sunny morning after that I would look forward to seeing my new good-morning friend outside our iron gate. A few days later I could not contain my curiosity any longer. Since I could not ask the man himself, I decided to ask Papa.

"Papa, do you know if a new family moved in down the street?"

"Why?"

"Well, I have seen this kind man every morning. He must walk this way to work. He always looks so sad."

"Oh?"

"I asked Fumi-san, and she told me it would be wrong to ask him. So I thought you might know who he is."

"Joya, I will look into it."

"Thank you, Papa!" I hugged him and went off to my room to put my bathing suit on for my morning swim.

I was in the koi pond when Papa came over to Fumi-san and I heard him say, "I am changing my schedule so I can be with Yuriko-chan in the morning." He then turned to me and asked, "Joya, does that sound like a good idea to you?"

"Oh, yes, Papa!" I was so happy to have extra time with Papa that it was a week before I realized that I had not seen the man again since Papa changed his schedule. He must have been visiting someone in our village, because I never did see him again.

As I finished my journal project, the principal announced the end of the school day.

CHAPTER FOUR

*"NEIGHBORHOOD ASSOCIATIONS' REMINDER—
WASTE NOT, WANT NOT UNTIL WE WIN!"*

Showa 19 August 27, NHK Radio Sunday show

The doorbell rang, and I knew it had to be Sumiyo-san arriving for dinner. I pinned back the stray hairs from my braids and went downstairs to greet her.

"Konnichiwa, Sumiyo-san. It is so nice to have you in our home," I said and then bowed to her.

"Good afternoon, Yuriko-chan. It is so nice to see you again and to be welcomed in your home," Sumiyo replied, bowing in return.

Papa motioned for Sumiyo to enter the dining room. As she walked away I noticed that the vivid red chrysanthemums embroidered on her kimono seemed to dance against the light peach silk. Sumiyo-san's long shiny hair was swept up in a chignon. She embodied everything I had read that an elegant Japanese lady should be.

Papa linked his arm with mine and walked me to the table. Once we sat, the maid brought out our dinner—chicken teriyaki served with shrimp and vegetable tempura.

"Yuriko-chan, how is your school year going?" Sumiyo-san asked.

I finished chewing before I replied. "It is going well, but there is so much homework to do."

"Ah, yes, I have heard that from my nieces as well. They are about your age and have so much schoolwork every night."

Sumiyo-san began to discuss what she had done in Kyoto when she had moved there a few years ago. I wasn't really paying attention, but I did notice the way she smiled at Papa whenever he spoke. It was not just a polite smile, but more of a loving glance. And he was smiling back at her in a similar way. I was not used to Papa looking at other people with such emotion. Something was different at this visit with Sumiyo-san, and I didn't like it.

"Yuriko-chan?" Papa's voice brought me back to the conversation.

"I am sorry, Papa. What did you say?"

"Would you like dessert?"

"Oh, no, thank you. I am full and still have homework. Would you please excuse me?"

"Of course, Joya."

I got up from the chair, turned to Sumiyo, and said, "It was a pleasure to see you again." I forced a smile as I bowed.

"Arigato, Yuriko-chan. I hope to see you again soon." She stood and bowed in return.

I went straight into my room. My futon was already made up for the evening. I sprawled out on top of it. Maybe I was just imagining that Papa had looked at Sumiyo-san differently. It was the first time we had seen her in a while. Maybe he was just being kind. It was a thank-you dinner and nothing else. Yes, that was all.

● ● ●

I had been staring at the same math problem for half an hour. I was having trouble concentrating, which was unusual because math was my favorite subject. I liked it so much because mathematics was black and white. It was one of the few things that always made sense.

A siren wailed suddenly, and I jumped. Another air raid drill. I reached over for the helmet laying by the side of my futon, placed it on my head, and strapped it under my chin. I was already wearing my belt secured with my ration and first-aid pouch. The Neighborhood Association (NA), set up by Japan's Home Ministry Department of Government, had told us two years ago that we must have it with us at all times. During the day, I kept it in my school bag. Papa told me to wear it while I slept so that it would take me less time to evacuate when there was a siren in the middle of the night. Because of it, I had to sleep on my back, which I hated. Some nights I slipped the belt off in my sleep so I could lie on my stomach, which was my favorite position on my futon.

"Joya, come now. Move faster!" Papa's voice boomed as he slid open my shoji and then went to Genji's room.

"I *am* moving fast, Papa." I should have been asleep an hour ago and my lids felt heavy. Besides, we went through these drills so many times that it was hard for me to have a sense of urgency. When the air raid drills first started a couple years ago, it was mostly for citizens to practice putting out fires from a bomb. Someone from each household had to go outside with a bucket and pass it down the line to put out an imaginary fire. The government asked us to practice this at school as well. Once, actual bombs dropped in 1942 and the greatest damage came from falling flakes of fire, so some of us practiced extinguishing flames by using a broom. The end of the broom had a water-soaked rope tied around it, which we flailed at the pretend flakes. It seemed more like a game.

Recently, sirens mostly alerted us that planes were overhead or that planes might be coming our way. We could be cooped up for as little as three minutes to a couple hours before the all clear was sounded.

Just as Papa came by my room a second time, I stepped out into the hall. He grabbed my hand and we headed to our shelter.

I hated being in the air raid shelter. When Papa started having it built, I imagined hidden tunnels and a room with a tatami floor and a hibachi. Instead, the shelter only had a small dirt floor that pooled with water infested with mosquitoes after any rain storm.

A voice from a megaphone penetrated the darkness. "There is still light showing in your window. Please be so kind as to fix that by the next air raid drill, Ishikawa-san." Our neighbor, Matsu-san, co-chaired the NA with Aunt Kimiko in our section of town. At night, her responsibility was to ensure that all the houses had their blackout curtains drawn. During the day, Matsu-san watched the skies for enemy planes. I was also convinced that she was spying on all of us.

As usual, I had to go to the bathroom. "Papa, I—"

He did not let me finish my sentence. He knew what I was going to say. "Yuriko-chan, I have a solution for you." Then he pointed to a bucket in the corner. Suddenly waiting until after the all-clear siren sounded didn't seem so impossible.

CHAPTER FIVE

*"A REMINDER FROM THE NEIGHBORHOOD
ASSOCIATION ON THIS THURSDAY MORNING:
PLEASE BE SURE BLACK OUT CURTAINS ARE
DRAWN EACH EVENING..."*

Showa 19 September 21, NHK Radio

On my walk home from school, I passed two women whispering about new ration books and the NA's fire bucket brigade drills only happening once a week now instead of three times a week.

The women's conversation reminded me of how I had begged Papa to let me participate in the bucket brigade. I finally wore him down and he agreed. The best times were when he would come out and do the drills with me. It was fun trying to get the water to the front of the lines first.

A horn blasted me out of my daydream. I nearly walked in front of a bus that turned the corner of my street. While I waited for it to pass, my eyes watered instantly, and I began to cough. I wished we had gasoline again. As I tried to wave away the smoke from the bus's coal engine, a woman approached me.

"Would you please sew on a stitch for my husband?" she asked.

"Yes, of course." I bowed and sewed an uneven red stitch on her thousand-stitch belt. These belts were given to a person's loved one before they left to fight for the Emperor. The belt encouraged the soldier, because he would know that one thousand women had faith in him to lead Japan to victory.

The woman bowed in return and said, "Thank you. I need five more people to sew a stitch and then I will have my one thousand stitches. I should be able to present this belt to my husband before he ships out at the end of the week. I will rest a little easier knowing this belt protects him while he is away."

I nodded and walked away. I was five years old when I first saw women on the corners asking passersby to sew a stitch for them on a piece of material. At the time, it seemed quite unusual. But, now, seven years later, it was so common that if I was daydreaming I might walk right past these women without even noticing them.

Approaching my house, my best friend, Machiko, waved me over. I never had any friends before I went to elementary school, and I didn't have a best friend until I met Machiko. Most of the kids in elementary school knew each other from their neighborhoods. But because Papa sheltered me, I didn't know any of them and immediately felt like an outsider. Eventually, a couple girls sat with me at lunch but they never asked me to do anything with them after school. Mostly they wanted to know who came to our big parties or what it was like to have a chauffeur.

One day, I was turning the corner and overheard one of the girls say, "Yes, my mother told me to be nice to her, too, because of her papa." I ate alone after that and kept to myself.

Until three years ago. I was walking to school and Machiko's younger brother came up to me, and he began to make fun of the way I had run from Taro-san and the rat snake. Machiko scolded him and made him apologize. She and I started sharing stories about her little brother and my cousin Genji and how annoying little boys could be. After that we were friends. I could that tell she liked me for me and not just for my family's status or money.

Machiko's mother worked at home, taking in clothing and doing alterations. Some nights when I visited after school, I helped Machiko put labels on the clothes. Whenever I helped, I was invited to stay for dinner. The food was always simple, but we had so much fun eating at the same table. It was nothing like the formal dinners we had at our house, where we ate mainly in silence.

"Machiko-chan, I missed you today! How are you?" I asked as I walked up the drive to Machiko's house.

"I'm fine. I had to stay home and watch my little brother

while my mother worked. But did you hear about the Watanabes?" Machiko said, a hint of sadness to her voice. The Watanabes were our longtime neighbors and a nice family.

"No—what about them?"

"Jiro-san received a red card." I stopped walking toward her. A red card meant that the Emperor had called the Watanabe's son to join the army and fight for Japan. It was supposed to be an honor but most of us knew it meant the possibility of never seeing a loved one again.

My eyes must have bulged from my head a little. "That's terrible! His mother must be so sad."

Machiko nodded and said, "His mother is coming around with his sash for people to add a stitch to for good luck. Watanabe-san came to our house earlier today. I'm sure she'll stop by your house soon."

Machiko tapped the spot on the porch step next to her, motioning for me to sit. "Yuriko-chan," she whispered, "I'm sad and scared for Jiro-san."

"Hai," I whispered back, nodding my head in agreement. Then I motioned for us to go inside. I had recently heard a rumor that one of our neighbors had been brought in for questioning at the local government office because he was speaking out against the war. Since then, I was extra careful when broaching the subject, convinced that there were spies everywhere.

Once we were safely in Machiko's room, she turned and asked, "When you were walking home, did you notice the new signs posted on Main Street?"

"No, I was daydreaming again."

"Well, if you *were* paying attention, you would have seen that the signs show a woman with a western wavy hairstyle and an X through it. Women are to sacrifice for victory and not be vain. But my father said last night that there is another reason, too." Machiko moved in closer and whispered in my ear, "The government does not want anything American here anymore. That includes any jazz records! This morning, my father told me I should dispose of them. Can you believe it? How can music be banned? It sounds so pretty. Why is that bad?"

A sinking feeling overcame me. I hadn't heard about any of this. My Aunt Kimiko still styled her hair in western curls. I made a mental note to tell her about the new order *in front* of Papa later, so she'd be sure not to tell me I'm being disrespectful. But what was wrong with jazz music? That didn't make any sense.

"Our kabuki music sounds like ghosts moaning in a haunted shrine!" I said. I began to imitate one of the famous kabuki actors with exaggerated facial expressions and groaning as if in pain. Machiko and I laughed so much we had a hard time catching our breath.

Suddenly, Machiko looked very serious, "Yuriko, I have to confess something."

"What?" I asked.

"Well . . ." She paused, looked around, cupped her hand

around my ear, and whispered, "I kept one of my jazz records anyway, but Papa doesn't know."

My eyes widened.

"I just couldn't give it up. It's my favorite. Who can I harm by listening to it in my room alone?"

"I don't think that's really bad, but I'm just surprised you did it. You usually follow the rules no matter what. This is a different side of you—I like it!" I patted her on the back, and her shoulders slumped in relief. "We'll listen to it together sometime, but I should get home now." I stood and we walked silently to the entryway, where I slipped my shoes back on.

"Sayonara, Yuriko. See you tomorrow," Machiko said with a slight smile.

"Sayonara, Machiko." And turning, I headed down the drive, crossed the street to my house, humming my favorite jazz song in my head.

CHAPTER SIX

"We Must Defend to the End on All Sides of Japanese Empire, Our Floating Castle."

Showa 19 September 21, NHK Radio

I crossed the street and walked the short way to my front door. I began my ritual of kicking my shoes off in the entrance hall. I didn't like to stop and put them away in a neat row. I had to be so proper all day at school, and I refused to do it at home, at least when I could help it. I shoved my book bag into the coat closet. The blackout curtains were drawn, and my eyes had to adjust to the lone glow of the shoji lamp. I walked with caution down one side of our stone-floor hallway, as the other side would still be wet from its afternoon cleaning. Aak! My right sock slid on the damp floor. I'd chosen the wrong side.

As I bent down to take off my soggy sock, I heard Papa in his study. As I drew closer, I saw that his door was slightly ajar. Through it, I saw Watanabe-san bow and thank him. She turned and almost bumped into me. I noticed her eyes were red and puffy as she bowed to me. I knew that we were supposed to say the standard "How happy we all are that her son had received this honor." But I didn't want to lie, so instead I just bowed.

Many families came to visit my papa to ask for help in planning their chohei pati, a celebration party to send their sons off to war. I never understood why it was called a celebration. The event was not joyful as relatives and neighbors gathered to commemorate the soldier's life—in case he might not return home alive. My papa was very gracious and usually funded these parties. He'd also find extra rations for the party's meal. Because Papa funded these parties, we had to attend each one in our neighborhood. I didn't like going because they were so sad, but I had no choice.

"Hello, Papa," I greeted him, giving him a hug.

"Joya! Welcome home. How was school?"

Seeing Watanabe-san and hearing of her son's red card, I had almost forgotten the news about my teacher.

"Papa, Yakamura-sensei was not at school today," I said, waiting for his reaction.

He nodded his head, then said, "I see. Well, it is for the best."

He didn't seem surprised. I knew he wouldn't be as excited as I was, but I had hoped to get more of a reaction—or an explanation about his phone call yesterday. But instead, Papa changed the subject. "Joya, I am going to take my bath, and then I will do your hair on the veranda tonight."

"Yes, Papa. I will get a piece of fruit and meet you upstairs." Papa had to help me with my hair. Unlike Machiko or the girls in my class, my hair was dry and wiry like my cousin Genji's. In order for it to look presentable, Papa had to brush warm oil through it then wrap it in a towel. The process took about an hour. After that, he brushed it out again and pulled it into braids. Aunt Kimiko tried to take over fixing my hair when she first moved in after her divorce, but I put up such a fuss that she never tried again.

"Yuriko-chan, is that you?" Aunt Kimiko called out from the kitchen.

"Hai."

"I want to remind you that the Gofuku salesman will be here tomorrow afternoon. We will be ordering our special kimonos for Oshagatsu, the New Year celebration, and Sakura Hanami, the Cherry Blossom Festival. Make sure you are not late tomorrow!"

I nodded, choosing a plum from the fruit basket and rolling my eyes as I left the kitchen. Gofuku was a specialty store for kimonos. Most people went to the shop itself to buy very beautiful ready-made kimonos for the New Year or Cherry Blossom festivals. But since Papa was a prominent business owner, the storeowners came to our home instead to entice us with all the newest silk designs. I didn't enjoy wearing kimonos because I had to be wrapped so tightly and walk with such dainty steps. But I loved looking at the bolts of pretty fabric that the sales people laid out for us when they visited.

I went upstairs and sat on the veranda to finish my plum while I waited for Papa. I put my feet up on the wicker table, something I would never try inside for fear of Aunt Kimiko yelling at me, and wiped the plum juice from my hands onto my skirt.

I noticed a scraping noise coming from our yard below. I stood on my tiptoes and leaned over the veranda's railing. It was dusk, and my eyes strained to see clearly, but it looked as if some men were standing below, digging something with shovels.

"Konnichiwa!" I shouted. They looked up and waved, then left the yard abruptly.

"Joya, what is so interesting down there?"

I jumped. "You startled me, Papa."

"I am sorry. I did not mean to."

"Papa, there were some men down there digging."

"Oh, yes. I thought I would plant more shrubs. It is getting late so I guess they will be back tomorrow to finish."

I gave him a puzzled look. It was an odd time to be planting anything in the yard—we'd never done that this late in the season before.

I moved toward Papa so he could brush the oil through my hair. It took a long time, and tonight he wasn't as talkative as usual.

"Is something wrong, Papa? You are so quiet tonight," I finally asked in barely a whisper.

He sighed. "Joya, some days I am discouraged by the news I print about the war."

"But Japan is winning the war. How can that be discouraging?" I swiveled my body so he could brush the other section of my hair.

"A few years ago I believed we were winning, but now I am not so sure," Papa said solemnly.

I felt a chill travel up my spine to the nape of my neck. Victories were reported daily at school. I never thought that losing the war was even possible. I turned to face Papa and stammered as I asked, "So . . . Japan could lose?"

He pushed the bangs out of my eyes and said, "We have been fighting for seven long years. Our army supplies have been drained." He helped twist me back around and continued to brush my hair.

"What do you mean, Papa?"

"Well, for one thing we need to build more planes but have no metal to do that with."

I knew that we had no metal to use at school, but I hadn't thought that the government could have also had a shortage that would stop them from manufacturing planes.

"Is that why Matsu-san came by yesterday, to collect whatever spare metal we had laying around the house?"

"I did not know she had come yesterday. Who did she speak with?"

"Aunt Kimiko. She told Matsu-san to stop by once you were at home."

"Well, I will deal with Matsu-san later. War is not something we need to keep discussing, Joya. I want to hear about your day." He finished wrapping my hair in a big towel. We both took a seat on the wicker bench, and put our feet up on the table.

My nerves would not be subdued. It frightened me to think our country could be on the losing side of the war. Before I could stop myself, I asked, "Papa, what would happen to us if Japan lost the war?"

"I will keep my family safe at all costs. Know this, Joya—you are my life and I will give mine to save yours."

"Papa, do not talk that way. I do not want to be here if you are not." I felt tears building in my eyes and leaned my head to rest on Papa's shoulder, squeezing his hand.

He squeezed back and said, "But that is how life is, Yuriko-chan. In our lives we must experience both beginnings as well as endings. It is like the season changing after the last cherry blossom falls."

CHAPTER SEVEN

*"NEIGHBORHOOD ASSOCIATIONS TO DELIVER
FOOD RATION TICKETS TOMORROW."*

NHK Radio Friday morning broadcast

Just as I was getting ready for school, an air raid warning sounded. I eagerly gathered my supplies and ran to the shelter near our home. An early morning air raid usually meant school would be canceled. Papa had gone into work early, so he was the only one not in the shelter from our family. Three minutes later, the all clear sounded. After we got back inside the house, the radio announcer confirmed that there would be no school today.

"Yay!" Genji and I said in unison. For once, I could agree with him on something.

As I finished up my breakfast Aunt Kimiko came into the kitchen and said, "Gofuku's will be here to show us the kimono fabric in an hour since there is no school. Make sure you are here and not at Machiko's! Also, we will only be purchasing one kimono to use for both Oshagatsu and Sakura Hanami. "

"Yes, Aunt Kimiko." That was odd. I wondered why this year we'd only be ordering one kimono to share for each festival. We usually got a separate kimono for each.

I went into the study to read. Fumi-san entered a little while later, and said, "Yuriko-chan, Gofuku's just arrived and are setting up in the dining room. Kimiko-san said you have five minutes before you need to meet with them."

"Thank you, Fumi-san. I will finish my chapter and go right in."

Fumi-san nodded and left.

I finished reading the last paragraph on the page of *Botchan* and returned the book to its spot on the bookcase, and went to wash my hands before I handled the expensive fabric. Just as I finished, I heard Aunt Kimiko calling my name. I rushed to the dining room.

I greeted the seamstress and was immediately in awe of the beautiful bolts of red, pink, and indigo fabrics displayed on our dining room table. Some of the fabrics had a luxurious silky feel to them. Others had a brocade weave design. After much back and forth, I finally decided on a silky red and orange fabric. The fabric's decorations were gold cherry blossoms and maple leaves. Aunt Kimiko chose an indigo silk fabric with a bamboo and plum blossom design.

I managed to stand still long enough for the sales person to take my measurements and was greatly relieved when it was all over. I returned to my book in the study where it would be quiet.

"Yuriko-chan! Please read a story to your cousin. I need you to watch him while I run some errands," Aunt Kimiko yelled from the entryway, slamming the front door behind her.

I rolled my eyes as I heard Genji's footsteps pounding down the stairs. Well, the quiet was nice while it lasted. I sort of wished I'd had school after all.

CHAPTER EIGHT

"Imperial Japanese Navy Takes a Different Strategical Tactic on Island of Angaur."

Showa 19 October 22, NHK Radio Sunday morning news

My fists tapped my legs as I paced around the sewing machine, which was set up in the living room. I mumbled to myself, "How could you be so foolish and wait so long to finish this?"

"Yuriko-chan, may I help you?" a pleasant voice asked.

I came to a halt, looked up, and saw Sumiyo-san standing in the doorway. I'd forgotten she was coming early today for Sunday dinner. I rubbed the back of my neck. *How long has she been watching me?*

"Good afternoon, Sumiyo-san. I have to finish my sewing assignment for school tomorrow." A burning sensation traveled from my ears to my face.

"How much do you have left to do?"

My shoulders sagged. "Well . . . all of it."

Sumiyo-san nodded. "I see." She walked over to the sewing machine and sat down. "Please," she said, patting the seat next to her. Once I joined her she asked, "So, what is this sewing project, Yuriko-chan?"

"I am supposed to make a baby kimono." I sighed.

"I see. Well, do you know how to do the stitches to make a kimono?"

I looked down and wiped my sweaty palms on my skirt. "No, Sumiyo-san."

She lifted my chin and said in a soft voice, "Then let me show you how to make the satin stitches with this machine. It is tricky at first, but I know you can learn."

Looking at her, I realized that when Sumiyo-san smiled, her eyes lit up as well—just like Papa's did when he looked at me. Aunt Kimiko never looked at me that way.

Her graceful hands began to push the delicate fabric through the sewing machine, while I watched carefully. "Now, you can try." When she switched places with me, she guided my clumsy hands to move the material and to stitch the kimono.

"I am sewing!" I exclaimed.

Sumiyo-san clapped her hands and replied, "Of course you are. You can do anything if you try, Yuriko-chan."

Time sped by and for the first time ever one of my sewing assignments actually looked like what it was supposed to be. Our maid came in and announced that dinner was ready. Before we walked into the dining room, I turned to Sumiyo-san. "Thank you so much for your help. I could not have finished the kimono without you."

She touched my arm and said, "I was happy to help, Yuriko-chan. You did a wonderful job."

I didn't know what else to say, and there was an awkward silence until she spoke again. "We should go to the dining room. Your papa will be waiting." She took my hand and we walked in together.

My good mood vanished when I saw Aunt Kimiko, Genji, and a man I didn't recognize seated at our dining room table along with Papa.

The man stood and Papa introduced us. "Yuriko-chan, this is Akira-san. He is my best reporter."

"It is nice to meet you," I said and bowed.

He replied, "A pleasure to meet you as well." He bowed in return.

During dinner, Akira-san was seated next to Aunt Kimiko. Toward the end of the meal, Genji blurted out, "Akira-san, can we play ball after we eat like we do at your house?"

My aunt's cheeks turned a shade of pink. Akira-san cleared his throat and said, "Yes, but you must eat all your dinner first."

"I will!" Genji said, and he saluted.

For weeks now, Aunt Kimiko and Genji had been disappearing every Sunday. I hadn't cared where they were, because it meant Papa and I had some time alone together, but now it all made sense.

"Yuriko-chan, what is your favorite subject at school?" Akira-san asked.

"Recess!" Genji chimed in and laughed at his own joke.

I glared at him. "I like math, and there's a journal project that we're working on this year that has been fun," I said.

"Ah, journal writing. Maybe you will be a reporter like your papa someday?" Akira-san suggested.

Papa beamed and patted my shoulder.

"Yes, I might," I said quietly in return. I loved to write, but I really had no interest in being a reporter. However, I always agreed when someone suggested it, because I knew Papa hoped one day I would be.

After dinner, I excused myself from the table. During the meal, I watched Aunt Kimiko as she gave me fake smiles, spoke politely, and laughed at all of Akira-san's jokes. It made me lose my appetite for dessert. And besides, I had to finish my journal assignment before bedtime:

Seven years ago, my mother got sick during the summer. I rode the train for the first time the day when Papa and I went to visit her in the hospital. My mother's room looked more like a hotel suite. It did not look like the army hospital that my dance class had visited to entertain the wounded soldiers. The soldiers had been in one large room with twenty cots lined up against each wall.

My mother had two rooms that were connected. Four of the soldier hospital rooms could have fit into her two rooms. When we first arrived, Papa sat on one side of her on the hospital bed and I sat on the other. Papa talked to Mama about what was happening at the newspaper office and in our neighborhood—gossip that he learned from our maid.

After that, I recited a few lines of her favorite Basho haiku that I had memorized, or I made up my own stories to make her laugh. A nurse served us dinner in her room. We pretended we were all out at a restaurant instead of at the hospital.

Papa and I stayed overnight. He slept in the connecting bedroom. I slept on the sofa in my mother's room. We stayed with her for three days, and then Papa decided to bring her home with a private nurse. She died one month later.

Each Sunday during that first year, Papa and I walked across the Hijiyama Bridge to visit her at the cemetery. We always stopped in the middle of the bridge and looked at our reflections below. One Sunday, Papa asked, "Joya, will you come every day to visit me when I am gone?" I could not even imagine such a time. He had to always be there, forever. However, I knew what to say and answered with an obedient yes.

I closed my journal. I didn't have many memories of my mother, but that visit at the hospital was the most vivid. I reached for a tissue to wipe the tears from my eyes just as my door slid open, startling me.

"Yuriko-chan, I wanted to tell you—" Genji stopped midsentence when he noticed I was wiping my eye. "Are you sad?" he continued. "Poor baby. Is it because your papa is downstairs with the lady he will marry?"

I scowled at him and slipped the hand that was holding

the tissue under my futon. "You are a liar, Genji! My papa is not getting married to Sumiyo-san. You are just a child. What do you know? And, I'm not crying!"

"Your papa is getting married," Genji sang as he left my room.

Oooh! I balled up my tissue and threw it at the door. Genji had just said that to make me mad. That was all. But when I thought about it, Sumiyo-san *had* been visiting every Sunday for the past two months. She blushed whenever Papa spoke to her. His eyes softened when he looked at her. Papa's driver picked her up and then Papa would drive her home. Could Genji be right?

As I got ready for bed I decided to talk with Machiko tomorrow about this fear on our walk to Jiro-san's chohei pati. Talking to Machiko usually helped me figure things out and I was sure this was all just a huge misunderstanding.

CHAPTER NINE

*"Unshakable Air Defense,
Immovable Front."*

Propaganda poster

I knocked on Machiko's door. She opened it and said, "Ohayo, Yuriko."

"Ohayo. I thought we could walk to Watanabe-san's house together."

"Let me tell my mother before we go!" she called, disappearing into the house and then returning, closing the door swiftly behind her.

We walked in silence until the end of the street. Finally, Machiko asked, "What is bothering you, Yuriko? Usually you are happy when we get to miss class." Because these send-offs signified such an honor bestowed to the young men, children could miss school for such events—that was really the only good thing about them.

But Machiko knew me so well. I took a deep breath and said, "Genji said something last night that upset me."

"He always says something to upset you," Machiko replied with a little laugh.

"Yes, but this time it really upset me. It was about Sumiyo-san and Papa."

"What about them?"

"Genji said that Papa is going to marry Sumiyo-san!" I began to tap my fists against my legs, which I did whenever I was nervous or angry.

Machiko stopped and turned to me. "Do you think it's true?"

"Well, she has been over every Sunday and she looks at Papa in a way that makes me uncomfortable. Sometimes Papa looks at her like that, too." I dropped my head.

"Is she still nice to you?" Machiko asked.

"Yes. She even helped me with my sewing project. But I usually go up to my room immediately after dinner. I don't like being around Papa when she's there." We continued walking.

"Hmm. Have you asked your papa about Sumiyo-san and if what Genji said is true?" she finally said to break the silence.

"No, not yet. If it *is* true, I don't want to know."

"Yuriko, you have to ask him. Why not do so this Saturday when you both go into the city?"

Saturday seemed too soon. But it would be better than not knowing. "I guess you're right."

"Of course, I am. If wondering about him and Sumiyo-san is making you so miserable, it would be better to know for certain. That way you can be miserable with a good reason." Machiko giggled as she put her arm around me.

"That makes sense." I laughed, too.

We arrived at Watanabe-san's house.

"Look at all the people who are here!" Machiko gasped.

"There is a lot of food, too. Earlier this morning Aunt Kimiko and the rest of the women in the NA set up tables with mochi cakes, kasutera, and tea."

As we approached the yard, I noticed a photographer taking a picture of Watanabe-san and her son, Jiro, under the shade of the ginkgo tree. I had learned, at the first chohei pati I'd attended, that this last family portrait was taken in case the son died while fighting for Japan.

"Jiro-san looks much older in his army uniform than he did when he was a mechanic covered in grease stains. Jiro-san actually looks quite handsome," Machiko said, her cheeks flushing a bit.

"I suppose. At least with the military haircut, his hair is out of his eyes. He would look better if he was smiling, though."

"His mother is not smiling, either. Anyone can see by her swollen, red eyes that she has been crying. My heart breaks for her." Machiko let out a small sigh.

"Mine does, too. I know I would never stop crying if Papa had to leave and fight in the war. And poor Watanabe-san. She's already lost her husband in the war and now her only son is leaving, too. Aunt Kimiko told me that some parents keep locks of their sons' hair, so if a son dies in battle and his body cannot be returned, the family has something to bury. Do you think Watanabe-san did that, too?" I wanted to think of Jiro's hair being in his eyes instead of in a box in the ground.

Machiko brought her hand to her chest. "Maybe she has."

"Why don't we have a cup of tea while we wait for the picture to be taken and then we can go give our good wishes to Jiro-san."

The tea tasted good while we waited. We finished just as the photographer began putting away his equipment. Watanabe-san went inside to bring out the sake for the final toast the adults would give to Jiro-san. We set down our cups and walked over to him.

"Hello, Jiro-san," Machiko and I said together. Machiko giggled and her cheeks turned pink.

Jiro-san gave us a shy smile. "Hello, Machiko-san and Yuriko-chan."

Hmm. Why did he refer to Machiko as an adult and me as a young girl? And why is Machiko so quiet and blushing? I had some questions for Machiko the next time we were alone. But to end the awkward silence with the three of us, I said, "We each stitched on your thousand-stitch belt."

"Arigato gozaimasu. So very kind of you." Jiro-san glanced at Machiko and then bowed. "Excuse me, but I must gather my things before the toast."

"Yes, of course. I wish you much luck, Jiro-san," Machiko said and then bowed.

"Yes, so do I." I gave him a smile.

As he walked away I turned to Machiko and said, "What was that all about?"

"What do you mean?" She blushed again.

But before I could continue, Watanabe-san approached and said, "Have you girls signed the good-luck flag for Jiro-san yet?"

"Oh, no. We will do it now," I replied.

Machiko and I walked over to the rising sun flag arranged on the table where the mochi cakes sat earlier. We wrote our names and *Ganbatte, Kudasai* on the flag. There were so many good-luck wishes, we barely had enough space to leave our own.

The older men from the Veterans' Association entered the yard wearing the army's khaki uniforms. Their arrival signaled it was time for the final toast. Everyone became quiet. One of the veteran's took his cup of sake, raised it in the air, and said, "Banzai!"

The adults, including Jiro-san, raised their sake cups, and we raised our tea cups, replying with another, "Banzai!"

We began to line up for the procession to the shrine and train station. Papa came over to me and said, "Joya, I must leave now. I am needed in the copy room to ensure the paper goes out on time." He gave me a hug, then turned to Machiko and said, "Sayonara, Machiko-chan."

"Sayonara, Ishikawa-san," Machiko replied. Then we began to follow the rest of the people in line and Papa went in the other direction.

As we walked, neighborhood children on their way to school joined our procession. We turned into the Nigitsu Shrine and walked along the cement pathway lined with stone lanterns leading us to the immense cement torii. We bowed before we passed under the left side of the torii, walking by the cement lions on either side that guarded the shrine. The left lion had his mouth closed, keeping the good spirits in, and the one on the right had its mouth open, scaring away the evil spirits.

From there we went to the covered temizuya to purify ourselves by rinsing our hands and mouths using the wooden ladle and water, which was held in a stone basin. We climbed the stairs to the hall of worship's altar, Watanabe-san rang the bell to let the deities know we were there, and we all bowed twice. We prayed silently for Jiro-san's safe return, clapped twice, and gave a final bow.

We continued on to the train station nearby, waving our mini rising sun flags, which were passed out at the party, and sang "The Patriotic March." Once we were at the station, we lined up along the tracks. Jiro-san stood on the step of the train and gave his farewell speech: "I believe that to do battle and go to his death for his country is the dearest wish of every Japanese man. I will do my duty with no thought of coming back alive. Good-bye everyone."

Everyone applauded except Machiko and me. In fact, Machiko gasped. Even though Jiro-san may have meant it and wasn't just saying it because he had to, we could not bring ourselves to applaud such an eerie and dark sentiment. The veterans began chanting and we automatically joined in: "Jiro-san, BANZAI! Jiro-san, BANZAI! Jiro-san, BANZAI!" I looked over at Machiko again. Her eyes were wet, and she looked pale, as did Watanabe-san.

Jiro-san gave us one last brave smile and wave. We continued to clap until only the smoke from the train's engine was left behind.

Aunt Kimiko and the NA ladies walked Watanabe-san home. The rest of the crowd either went back to school or work. I intended to walk home with Machiko and to find out how long she had liked Jiro-san, since it was pretty obvious she did. I pulled her back in line, so the other people could get ahead of us.

"How long have you liked Jiro-san? Why did you never tell me before?"

Machiko stopped and looked at me with wide eyes. "What do you mean?"

"Machiko, you are blushing as we speak. I know you pretty well, too, *and* I'm not blind!"

She smiled shyly, linked her arm in mine, leaned her head towards mine, and whispered, "I've liked him for a while. But he doesn't know, and we are too young and now . . ." Her voice trailed off, and she took a handkerchief from her pouch. She stopped to dab her eyes, and I hugged her.

She cleared her throat and said, "So, what is your plan on asking your papa about Sumiyo-san?"

Another thing Machiko was good at: changing the subject.

CHAPTER TEN

"First Attack of Kamikaze Squadron Used on Leyte Island."

Showa 19 October 28, NHK Radio
Saturday morning report

I lived for the weekends when Papa did not have to work. We would go out together to a restaurant in the main section of town on Saturday nights. When Aunt Kimiko and Genji first moved in, I worried that they would be joining us on these outings. But Papa never invited them, and for that I was very grateful.

On this latest outing, I was especially happy that Aunt Kimiko and Genji never joined us, because I was not sure how to ask Papa about Sumiyo-san when we were alone. I finished my bath and put on a western blue silk dress. I placed my pink hat with the polka-dotted ribbon on my head. I looked in the mirror and turned from side to side. I wasn't particularly fond of this outfit, but Papa had given it to me for my last birthday and it was his favorite. So I wore it to make him happy. At least the hat hid my unruly hair.

Papa and I walked hand-in-hand to the station. We boarded a train to the Handori station in downtown Hiroshima.

"I love going into the city, Papa." I squeezed his arm as I gazed out the window. The houses from our neighborhood disappeared from view and were replaced by the tall city buildings of the Fukuya department store and the Shintenchi theater district.

"I do, too, Joya. I have made reservations for us at our favorite restaurant."

"Oh, I'm going to order the sukiyaki!" My mouth began to water at the thought of the thinly sliced beef, vegetables, and delicious broth served at the table.

I looked out the window again, but an argument waged inside my head. *Should I ask Papa about marrying Sumiyo-san while we are on the train? Or would during the meal be better? No, maybe I will ask when we are walking down Main Street. Will that be too public, though? I should have discussed this with Machiko when I—*

"Joya, is everything all right?" Papa said with a look of concern.

"What? Oh, yes. I was just daydreaming."

"What about?"

Here was my opportunity to finally ask the question. But just when I opened my mouth to confront him, the conductor announced our station stop. So I simply replied, "Nothing important, Papa. I cannot wait to spend the evening together, that is all."

We exited the train station and walked out into the street, where savory aromas of the various restaurants and noodle carts wafted in the air. Shoppers walked past us purposefully while juggling their purchases, though each week there seemed to be fewer and fewer packages for them to juggle. I opened my mouth a few times to ask Papa about Sumiyo-san, but each time I tried to speak, I couldn't get the words out. So we strolled in silence, smelling the scents and people-watching.

We arrived at our favorite restaurant and were ushered in by the owner, who was a good friend of Papa's. The owner nodded at me and said, "Yuriko-chan, what a lovely young lady you look like tonight." He turned to face Papa and continued, "You must be so proud, Ishikawa-san." He bowed, and we bowed in return.

His compliment made me stand a little taller as I walked with daintier steps toward our table. Once we were seated, the waiter came to take our order. Papa handed me the adult menu and said, "Choose the meal for us tonight, Joya."

I didn't even have to look at the menu, though. "I love the sukiyaki meal," I said. "That is what I would like to order." Papa nodded his approval. Within minutes the electric hot plate was brought to our table and a sizzling pan was placed on the burner. The pan had tender steak, tofu, and bean sprouts that bubbled in a delicious sweetened soy sauce. Although, each week the portions were noticeably smaller. I picked up my chopsticks to move the food around in the pan. A sputter of hot oil hit my hand.

"Ouch!" I cried out, and then quickly covered my mouth in embarrassment for speaking so loudly in a public place. I did not want to embarrass my papa.

But he just shook his head and smiled. He reached over and turned the burner off, saying, "Now, you can serve our food *safely*."

I filled both of our plates. I tried to emulate Sumiyo-san's grace as she served us at the table during her Sunday visits. As we ate, the soft chatter of adults at the other tables was a welcomed sound. At home, our meals were either too quiet on the nights Papa worked late, or too loud thanks to Genji's constant babbling.

"Joya, how is your journal project coming along? You must be enjoying it, neh?"

I put down my chopsticks, finished chewing, and said, "The journal has been one of the more fun projects this year. It is better than having to present in front of the class, which is what we did at the beginning of the year."

Papa smiled. "Yes, I am sure it is."

I thought to myself, *All right, just ask about Sumiyo-san. This is the perfect time.* I took a breath and just as I was about to ask Papa, the owner came back to the table and asked him about one of the articles in the paper yesterday. I finished my meal while they spoke. The owner finally left but so had my courage.

After our meal, we headed toward the chocolate confectionary for dessert. I could smell the rich scent of chocolate from two store windows away. When I was younger, I would run to the store. But now that I was trying my act like a young lady, I used dainty steps to move as fast as I could.

When we entered, I walked the length of the counter, eying the one row of candies. There used to be many rows of various caramels and other confections. However, because of sugar rationing, only squares of milk chocolate, dark chocolate, and green tea chocolate were on display to tempt shoppers.

Papa asked, "What will you choose for your special treat this evening?"

I tapped on the top of the glass cabinet and contemplated. I took one last look up and down the counter and replied, "One huge square of dark chocolate, please."

"Ah, you have made a good choice, Joya." Papa feigned surprise, even though I made the same choice every week.

I offered him some of my candy and he broke a piece off. I finished the rest as we window-shopped on our way back to the train station. We passed one of the signs Machiko had mentioned, the one banning western hairstyles. I pointed it out to Papa. "I think that Aunt Kimiko needs to know about this, because she is still wearing her hair in western curls."

"You are right. I had wanted to speak with her about that," Papa said flatly.

I felt smug knowing that Aunt Kimiko would be upset

when Papa mentioned to her that her hairstyle must be changed. I knew I shouldn't think like this, but for once I could watch Papa get upset with her instead of Aunt Kimiko getting *me* in trouble.

As we neared the station, I remembered and then instantly missed the regal electric lanterns beautifully sculpted like lilies that hung overhead, lighting up in succession. They illuminated the storefronts all along the street as dusk faded to darkness. They were taken down to be melted into bullets quite a few months ago. Now we all hurried home before the sun set, so we didn't really need the streetlamps anyway.

As soon as we boarded the train toward home, I knew it was my last chance to ask Papa about Sumiyo-san before the evening was over. I took my window seat and began to stare at the tracks across the way. I ran through different ways of starting the conversation in my head. I crossed my legs then uncrossed them. I tapped my fingers on the arm rest.

"What is the matter, Joya?" Papa's voice started me out of my thoughts.

"What? Oh, I am fine. Just trying to get comfortable." I worried that on the night I wanted to be most ladylike, my nervousness made me appear like a child. I took in a deep breath, turned to face Papa, and finally spit out, "Papa, are you going to marry Sumiyo-san?" My stomach did flip-flops as I waited for his answer. I should have asked the question before we ate dinner as now I was feeling a bit queasy.

His expression didn't change, but I noticed that he squared

his shoulders. "Why would you ask me that?"

"Well, she has been visiting us every Sunday for nearly two months. Genji also said something—not that he knows what he is talking about." I gave a halfhearted laugh.

Papa put his arm around my shoulders and said, "Joya, it has been some time since your mother died. She can never be replaced, of course. However, I feel that it is time I married again. Akira-san has asked Aunt Kimiko to marry him just last week. And Sumiyo-san and I have decided to get married on the same day at the beginning of November. After the wedding, we will all live together at our home."

November? The reporter in Papa believed in stating an answer honestly and directly, but even though I knew that was his approach to answering most questions, this time he surprised me. In the back of my mind I had known it was a possibility. But that was only a few weeks away. I wished I'd thought out some possible responses, though, because my mouth just hung open. The only thing I managed to say was, "Oh . . . that will be nice."

"It will be a good thing for our family, Joya." He pulled me close to him, and I placed my head on his shoulder.

As I watched the station disappear into the night, I pondered what he'd said. The more I thought about it, the more I realized it might be nice to have Sumiyo-san living in our home, unless it meant that Papa would no longer spend any time with me. Would Sumiyo-san change the way the household was run? Would she order me around like Aunt Kimiko?

And whatever did Akira-san see in Aunt Kimiko anyway?

• • •

Two weeks later, Sumiyo-san arrived for Sunday dinner as usual, and Papa and I greeted her in the hall. When she came in, she said, "Yuriko, I brought a book you might enjoy. It is about samurai marriage rituals. Since you are not a child anymore, I thought you might want to know what will be happening on the day of the wedding."

Sumiyo-san's gesture amazed me. She clearly thought of me as a young lady, not as a child. I found myself releasing a small smile. Ever since the day she helped me with my sewing project, there was something I'd been considering asking her, and now seemed like the right time. So I cleared my throat and said, "Sumiyo-san, would you want to join Papa and me in town next Saturday?" My voice wavered and sounded more like a whisper. It wasn't easy for me to ask her to join in on my special outing with my papa. But I wanted to show her and Papa that I approved of their marriage and saw her as a part of our family. Giving up one of my outings with Papa was the best way I could think of to tell her that I liked her, too.

Sumiyo-san hugged me. "That is very nice of you to ask." She looked at my face and my papa's before she replied. "I am very grateful for the invitation, but your outings are a special tradition for you and your papa. And traditions are important. A papa and his daughter need time together, neh? We can all go out another evening, though, if you like."

I closed my eyes and exhaled as I hugged her back. Sumiyo-san understood that time alone with Papa was important to me. I let out another deep breath. Papa could be married *and* I would not have to give up my time with him. Perhaps Papa being married really wouldn't be so bad after all.

CHAPTER ELEVEN

*"How to Distinguish Enemy Carrier
Based Planes"*

Showa 19 November 5, NHK Radio Sunday program

"Yuriko-chan, come here, please," Aunt Kimiko's singsong voice called to me. When she used her singsong voice—and so politely—she was really demanding that I run to her without delay. Just to annoy her, I took my time reaching her dressing room. She was supposed to help me get dressed for the double wedding ceremony, and I was resisting, mainly because I hated wearing kimonos. They were beautiful, but they had so many layers. By the time the kimono was in place, I always felt packed in as tightly as rice in a sushi roll. But I wasn't only stalling to spite Aunt Kimiko or because of the kimono. As much as I liked Sumiyo-san, I was not fond of change. Having both Sumiyo-san and Akira-san move in would be a *big* change.

I let out a long breath, trying to push those thoughts aside, and entered Aunt Kimiko's dressing room through the ornate mahogany wood carvings that decorated the transom above the silk-screened shoji. Tansu chests with their narrow drawers lined three walls and were filled with beautiful kimonos, some almost a century old. A large beveled mirror hung on one side of the room, and Aunt Kimiko was standing in front of it with her hands on her hips. Before she could scold me for taking so long, I said in *my* best singsong voice, "Kimiko-san, I am so sorry for being late."

"Never mind that. Come over here, and put on your juban."

As she slipped the first layers of the kimono over my head, I admired the sea of beautiful fabric that was my kimono, which had been laid out before me. I skimmed my fingers over the delicate gold threads outlining the cherry blossom design. I wondered if Aunt Kimiko knew that when I picked out the kimono fabric from Gofuku's that it would be worn at her and Papa's wedding in addition to the two upcoming festivals. I stuck out my arms and slid them into the silky work of art. The fabric felt soft and cool against my skin.

"Stop squirming and stand still, Yuriko."

"But you are wrapping the obi too tightly!" I exclaimed, attempting to take a breath.

"It is fine. I want to finish with your kimono so I can get ready. It is *my* wedding day, after all."

"And *my* papa's, too." I set my jaw, rolled my shoulders back, and stared at our reflections in the mirror.

"There, you are done, Yuriko-chan." Then she waved me out of her room.

I walked to the sunroom, hating the delicate, short steps the kimono forced me to take. Papa was listening to the news on the radio when I entered.

"Remember to abolish desire until victory!"

"Good morning, Papa. Oh! You look so handsome!" I said, gasping a bit.

Papa turned off the droning announcer. I shuffled over and hugged him. In his black ceremonial silk kimono with the family plum Mon—the samurai crest—on it, he resembled one of our samurai ancestors from the pictures on his desk.

"Joya, what a beautiful young lady you are. We shall have our picture taken in the garden and then the ceremony will start."

The small wedding ceremony took place in our dining room. The mahogany screens were open wide, so the dining room expanded into one large room looking out over the garden's fountain. Our relatives were seated on one side of the room facing Akira-san's family and Sumiyo-san's sister and nieces. Both my aunt and my soon-to-be stepmother were wearing white silk brocade shiromuku. The heavily embroidered over-robe had a scarlet lining and a padded hem so it trailed just a bit behind each of them. The shiromuku was worn over a plain silk white kimono with an obi and had gold embroidery outlining cranes, pine branches, and plum blossoms.

The only other color was the black eye of the crane. The left neckline fold had a white brocade pouch tucked in with two tassels showing. I found it quite interesting that in samurai times this pouch held a small dagger for protection. However, these days a good-luck charm has replaced the dagger. Papa had told me that this was a tradition of samurai families.

Sumiyo-san looked elegant, and even Aunt Kimiko looked pretty. Each wore a tsunokakushi, a white ceremonial headband, in her hair. As my papa had told me, in samurai days, the bride wore a white hood instead of the tsunokakushi "to hide a bride's horns." I almost laughed out loud wondering if Aunt Kimiko's horns were hiding somewhere.

The Shinto priest began the purification ceremony. Genji tapped me and asked, "What is that man doing with those sticks?"

I tried to ignore him, but he was persistent. I began to regret bragging to him about the book Sumiyo-san had given me last week, which explained all about a Shinto wedding ceremony—something I'd never seen before. I turned to him and whispered, "He is the priest and is performing the purification ceremony to bless the newly married couples and their families. Those sticks are from the sacred sakaki tree, and they are tied together with white linen streamers. See how he is waving the branch back and forth? That is how he blesses the married couple. Now, watch, and be quiet."

Soon after, the san san kudo ritual began. Genji threw me a puzzled look, so I whispered, "The grooms each have three small cups of sake. They take three sips from each cup and then hand them to the brides. After your mother and Sumiyo-san take three sips from each cup they will pass them to the families. But we do not get to drink any sake." Genji grunted, folding his arms across his chest, and stayed quiet for the rest of the ceremony.

After the ritual came my favorite part—the food! Fumi-san brought out lacquered trays with dishes of azuki bean rice, egg omelets, sushi cakes with smoked salmon, rice, and vegetables. For dessert she served delicious azuki mochi cakes!

For the meal, Sumiyo-san and Aunt Kimiko had each changed into a breathtaking red silk kimono with pairs of cranes, plum blossoms, chrysanthemums, and evergreens embroidered across the fabric. Their hair was now styled with lacquered combs and delicate flower kanzashi metal hair ornaments swaying daintily anytime they moved their head. My papa was seated at the head of the table with his bride. Aunt Kimiko and Akira-san sat next to them. Papa stood, raised his cup, and said, "Kanpai! Congratulations!"

I looked across the table and noticed Aunt Kimiko's face glowing. It was one of the few times I had seen her so happy. During the toast, Genji kept poking me with his chopstick. I had yet to understand why I had to be so delicate while he got to act like a monkey. At five years old he should behave better, but because he was a boy he got away with it.

"Kanpai!" we all shouted again. As I raised my glass of

juice, my elbow accidentally nudged Genji off his chair, but I made sure it was done in a *delicate* way.

CHAPTER TWELVE

"WITH THE COOPERATION OF JAPAN, CHINA, AND MANCHUKO, THE WORLD CAN BE AT PEACE."

Showa 19 November 12, Propaganda poster

I closed my book and turned off my lamp. I snuggled under the covers and heard muted voices coming from Genji's room. Akira-san was reading to Genji and something must have been funny, because I heard Aunt Kimiko's laughter, too. It had been a strange couple of weeks with two extra people in the house. As an only child, I hated sharing, especially my time with my papa. However, I found that the extra hushed voices and laughter comforted me *most* of the time.

I woke in the middle of the night. On my way to the bathroom I heard hushed voices again, but this time it was not Akira-san and Aunt Kimiko. I had never heard Sumiyo-san raise her voice to Papa, but tonight she was loudly whispering to him. I pressed my ear against the closed shoji and could barely make out her words.

"What are you doing? Where did you find him? And why would you bring him home?"

"I was walking back from the train station and found him on the side of the road. He was vomiting and coughing. I told him that he should go home. He told me he did not have one. I could not leave him there so sick. That would not be right."

"Where is he?" Sumiyo-san asked, and her voice faltered.

"He is in the kitchen eating some dinner. Afterwards, he will have a bath and sleep in the guest room."

"But the government says—"

"The government does not rule this household—I do." At that, I heard footsteps approach. I quickly ducked out of the way as Sumiyo-san emerged, walking to her bedroom, muttering about the stubborn man she had married.

I was curious, so I crept down the stairs and peered into the kitchen where I saw a young man's profile. He turned, and I saw why Sumiyo had been concerned—the young man was Korean.

My eyes opened wide and my cheeks burned, but I managed to say, "Hello. I am Yuriko."

"Hello, Yuriko-chan. It is nice to meet you. Your father is a very nice man. I am honored to be a guest in his home."

"Welcome to our house. You can have all the miso soup you want. That way *I* do not have to have it in the morning." I smiled at him, and he shot me a smile back in return.

I turned to go to my room but ran straight into Papa.

"Joya, a person of means has responsibility to others. Remember that." His hands rested on my shoulders.

"Yes, Papa, I will." My heart pounded in my chest. I did not expect to get caught spying.

"Good night, Joya." He turned my body in the direction of the stairs.

"Good night, Papa." I headed back to my bedroom. Once in bed, I remembered what woke me up in the first place and got up again to go to the bathroom.

Once back in my room, as I tried to fall back asleep, I could not stop thinking about our visitor in the kitchen. He looked kind to me. I was proud of my papa for not acting the same as everyone else. I'm not sure why Japan annexed Korea and used them as laborers in the deplorable conditions of the coal mines. Some kids in my class would speak as if the Koreans should be outcasts. I couldn't understand why Japanese people were considered better than Koreans. Weren't we all fighting on the same side in this never-ending war?

The next morning, when I went to wash my face, I noticed that our visitor was gone. It was also very quiet in the house. I put on some monpe pants and a shirt made from old kimonos. Aunt Kimiko made this shirt at one of her last neighborhood meetings. The government wanted women to wear monpe pants so they could run faster to the bomb shelters or to help maneuver pails of water in case of fire caused by bombs. Pants were much easier to move in than kimonos or western skirts, and I liked them because they were comfortable. Anything was better than the uniforms I had to wear during the week.

I went downstairs to the dining room for breakfast and found Sumiyo there, drinking her tea.

"Ohayo, Sumiyo-san."

"Ohayo. Yuriko, now that I am your papa's wife, please call me Sumiyo."

"Yes, of course, Sumiyo." I was pleasantly surprised.

Sumiyo smiled and squeezed my hand. I squeezed and smiled back.

"So, Yuriko-chan, did you sleep well?"

"Yes, I did, thank you." I could tell that she had not slept well, due to the dark circles under her eyes.

We ate our breakfast in silence. Well, it *was* silent until Genji came running through the dining room wearing a toy samurai helmet and singing, "Tenno heika banzai, Long live the Emperor!" He ran right past us and out the kitchen door into the garden.

Sumiyo attempted to muffle her laughter and said, "Yuriko, please excuse me. I need to go into town to do some shopping. I will see you when I return."

"Have a wonderful morning, Sumiyo." I was glad to see her smile again. I finished my breakfast and decided to read one of my books in the sunroom. As I settled into the wicker chair, Aunt Kimiko entered.

"Yuriko-chan, my NA meeting will be starting soon.

Remember, you are to help with assembling the care packages today."

"Yes, Aunt Kimiko, I remember." I rolled my eyes. She had only been reminding me about it for days.

I got up from the chair and heard Genji singing at the top of his lungs, "Kushu da, kushu da, air raid, air raid . . ."

It was such a terrible song, but since the war started, schools had started teaching it in kindergarten classes, to make sure even the youngest kids knew the importance of what they needed to do should the sirens sound.

●●●

Our dining room table was covered with magazines, candy, soap, razor blades, cigarettes, copies of my papa's newspaper, and letters for our troops. When the war started, we hoped these packages would remind the soldiers of home. All these years later, we hoped the soldiers would still be alive to enjoy them.

As I started to set up the boxes, our neighbors arrived, and they brought their own contributions for the war effort.

Machiko walked through the door with her mom, and I greeted them. Machiko pulled me aside and said, "Watanabe-san will be here soon. My mother and I offered to walk with her, but she wanted to wait for the mail to arrive."

"Ah. How is Jiro-san doing?"

"Well, she is really worried about him. She has not heard

from him in a few weeks. That may mean he is on the front lines." She hesitated, and then said, "I'm worried, too." Her brow furrowed as she tucked strands of hair behind her ear.

"I feel so bad for her, having her son away at war. Why don't we make a special card just for Jiro and mail it with a special comfort package?"

Machiko smiled. "That's a wonderful idea! Oh, look, here she is."

At that moment Watanabe-san walked in with red eyes that had dark shadows beneath them. She managed a smile when she saw us.

"Konnichiwa, Watanabe-san. Thank you for coming to the meeting. Machiko and I will be making a special card and package for Jiro-san this afternoon."

Her eyes lit up, and I think I saw some tears pooling in them. She took both Machiko's and my hand in hers. "Arigato gozaimasu. Such kind girls. He will be so happy knowing people are thinking of him back home. I haven't heard from him in a while, but I know he will like receiving your package."

Aunt Kimiko led Watanabe-san to the table with the other women. She gave us both an approving nod and smile. We headed over to our table and began loading up the packages.

While we worked, the older women chatted about upcoming lectures on gas masks and who might have cheated by receiving extra food rations. Machiko and I hummed one of the funny songs we learned at a dance recital we did years ago, which was put on for wounded soldiers. We had looked ridiculous in our samurai makeup and costumes for the recital. Since that day, we hummed this song whenever we wanted to make each other laugh.

We continued to hum and giggle until we had packed the last box, which was for Jiro-san. Sumiyo, who had returned from shopping hours ago, brought out our lunches. While we ate sushi and shrimp tempura, one of the women explained, "The soldiers need to know that they have strong stable families. It's important that we are frugal and give whatever we can to the military forces."

As she started to speak about gas masks, I began to daydream. I couldn't help myself. She was repeating what we had heard daily on the radio, and I was completely bored. I felt myself drifting away, thinking of our dance recital and of seeing my papa later that evening. Suddenly, someone poked my shoulder. It was Aunt Kimiko, and she gave me one of her looks of both anger and embarrassment. Machiko hid a sympathetic grin behind her hands.

Finally, the presentation ended, and I tried to slip out to Machiko's house with her.

"Yuriko-chan, remember you are to read to Genji before you go," Aunt Kimiko called after me just as I was exiting the front door.

"I thought I would read to him later tonight. I want to go to Machiko's house now."

"You can go afterward. Genji has been really looking forward to reading the latest *Norakuro*."

Machiko shot me a smile and said, "I'll stay with you while you read. I like the *Norakuro* anyway. Go, and get Genji."

I walked at a turtle's pace toward Genji's room, hoping he was still napping. Instead, I found him holding the comic book about the soldier dog in his hands. He chanted, "Norakuro, Norakuro."

"Come on. Let's go to the dining room, and I will read to you there."

Machiko and I sat on the floor on either side of Genji and began to take turns reading. We tried to see who could make a better dog voice.

"Private second class Norakuro reporting, sir. Woof, woof." Machiko used her best dog voice while saluting.

"No, I can do better than that!" I exclaimed. "Sir, I am ready to fight. The enemy's silly bullets won't hurt me. Rrrrruf!" I stood tall and puffed out my chest.

We were all laughing, and by the comic's end, I realized how much fun I'd actually had reading to Genji.

As I closed the comic, I patted my cousin on the head. Then Machiko and I snuck out of the house before Aunt Kimiko came up with something else she wanted done.

CHAPTER THIRTEEN

"Extravagance is the Enemy!"

Propaganda poster

Once we were at Machiko's, we headed upstairs and straight to her room. Her house was small, but because she had younger brothers, she had her own room. The boys slept in the living area at night.

Machiko closed the shoji door. "Shh," she said, motioning with her finger pressed to her lips. "Come here, Yuriko." I crept near her as she pulled her record player out from under the futon in her closet. She lifted up one corner of her tatami mat and slid out a record. The album cover had a famous kabuki actor on it. But it had to be the jazz record she was hiding inside—I just felt that it had to be. She pulled out the record and placed the needle on the first song. The volume was low, but the sound of a piano and trumpets instantly filled the room.

We began to softly snap our fingers and dance with the beat.

"You know, Yuriko, my papa heard that some of the cafés are playing jazz again, but they added in some Japanese folk lyrics to the songs. It's being called 'light music.' Some of the Kempeitai can't tell the difference."

"Well, you should still be careful anyway. I don't trust Matsu-san especially. I think she looks for people to report just so she seems more important than she is." I glanced out the window, then continued, "I don't understand why these songs can't be played on the radio. This music could build up national spirits better than the government's 'Be frugal!' slogans that are played on the radio instead."

"I agree," Machiko said.

"I can stay for a few more songs, but then I have to go home and finish my homework. Sorry."

"You always wait until the last minute to get your work done," Machiko said and shook her head. "Did your teachers tell you yet that this summer we will have to work for the war effort instead of joining our usual clubs? Although, most of the clubs have been suspended because of the war. But either way, what a horrible way to spend our summer!"

"No, my teachers never said anything about that. What kind of work?"

"I don't really know. My eldest brother heard that workers are needed in the plane factories. Children at those factories must live there, too. I hope we won't have to do that."

"Imagine having to leave home and work in a factory all summer!"

"Yuriko, your papa would never let that happen to you, I'm sure of it." Machiko reached over and gave my hand a small squeeze. But it only helped calm my nerves somewhat. *What would I do if they sent me away from home, away from my papa? What would I do if Machiko was sent away and I couldn't see her for weeks at a time?* As we listened to the quiet jazz as it filled the room, a small shiver crept up my spine.

CHAPTER FOURTEEN

*"The Imperial Air Training Army
Continues Successful Attacks
in the Marianas Islands."*

Showa 19 November 15, Wednesday edition

"Yuriko, it's time to go!" Genji pounded on my door, emphasizing each word with a louder knock.

"Stop banging! I'll be down soon!" I placed one last pin in my hair and slid my door open. Genji stood there still.

"Look," he said, "I am wearing hakama for the first time! Akira-san gave them to me. He and his brothers wore this same hakama when they celebrated Shichi-go-san!"

"Yes, Genji-chan, you look like every other five-year-old boy who will be wearing kimono pants for the first time at the shrine today." I pushed past him and went downstairs. He, of course, followed me.

He smirked and said, "You're just jealous that this day isn't about you!"

"Remember, this is for three- and seven-year-old girls, too, so I already had my day." Before I had a chance to say more, Akira-san entered the room.

"Genji-chan, you look very handsome in my family hakama," he said, and Genji puffed out his chest. But then Akira-san continued, "However, this ceremony is about showing respect for yourself and your family, and of honoring your heritage. So you should show respect for your older cousin." I turned toward Genji and raised my eyebrow. At that moment, Aunt Kimiko called Genji's name and he ran to her in the kitchen.

Suddenly I felt Akira-san's hand on my shoulder. "And the older cousin should set a good example for her younger cousin, too," he said chuckling and shaking his head at me.

"I'm sorry, Akira-san. But sometimes Genji makes me so mad." I crossed my arms over my chest.

"Yes, I understand. I had younger cousins, too. They can be difficult. But you need to set a good example for him."

"How did you do that for your younger cousins?" I asked, still pouting a bit.

"Well, even when they really annoyed me, I would not let them know it. Instead, I would go outside and throw pebbles into the pond near my home. Sometimes that helped. Our gardener had to keep replenishing the rocks in our garden after every visit!" He then winked at me. "I want you to know that you can come talk to me anytime, Yuriko-chan."

It was nice to know I could turn to someone other than Papa, especially someone as nice as Akira-san. When we went to the shrine to pray that good health would follow all the boys at the celebration, I also gave thanks for Akira-san being a part of our family.

At the shrine, the boom of a taiko drum opened the ceremony. A Shinto priest said a purification prayer that would keep all the young boys and girls safe from harm and handed out omamori, a wooden good-luck amulet inside a small brocade bag, to each boy and girl celebrating Shichi-go-san. A Miko, or shrine maiden, shook bells to bless the children. The priest explained that this had been done since samurai times to celebrate boys on their third, fifth, and seventh years of life and girls on their third and seventh years.

Genji received his omamori and ran off to a food cart. I followed him. "Remember not to open the bag! If you read your amulet, you will lose any good luck from it."

"Yes, I know. I want to be first in line to get my chitose ame." I didn't understand why he was so excited about the sugar stick candy. The only thing I liked about the thousand-year candy was the wrapper. It had beautifully drawn pictures of cranes and turtles—symbols for longevity. The candy itself tasted like flour paste mixed with just the tiniest bit of sugar. Since there were fewer rations of sugar, I figured it would be especially unappetizing this year.

Akira-san found us on our way to the cart and went with Genji to purchase the sweet. As we left the shrine, I watched

Genji and his friends as they walked in front of me doing their best impersonation of samurai warriors. They moved as if they were drunken sumo wrestlers. I had to wonder, why were boys, who acted like that, favored over girls? I shook my head and popped a piece of candy in my mouth.

CHAPTER FIFTEEN

"Announcement from Our Imperial General Headquarters, Japan has Taken a Great Sacrifice in the Philippines in Leyte Gulf, but This Sacrifice Will Lead to Japan's Victory."

Showa 19 December 31, NHK Radio Sunday show

"Joya, you must get up. We are going with Sumiyo and Aunt Kimiko to meet the ship with Watanabe-san," Papa said as he shook my shoulder.

"What? Is Jiro-san coming home? Was he wounded?" I asked. I sat up on my futon and pushed the hair out of my face.

"No, he was not wounded. We must be there with Watanabe-san when she"—he hesitated and his voice shook as he finished his sentence—"takes the remains of her son home."

I sank farther down in my futon. I never thought we would know someone who would die in the war. I had known there were casualties, of course. That's what happens when you go to war. But to be this close to death frightened me. Tears did not fall until I thought of Machiko and her feelings for Jiro-san. Papa took my hand, helped me up, and hugged me.

As we were leaving our house, I said to Sumiyo, "I need to go get Machiko before we go to the docks."

"Your Aunt Kimiko left the house earlier to tell Machiko's mother about Jiro-san." She paused and dabbed her eyes. "Machiko's mother was leaving the house to pick up medicine for her younger son, who is sick. Machiko was at home caring for him."

"She does not know about Jiro-san then?"

"No. She was fond of Jiro-san, neh?" Sumiyo smiled and touched my arm.

"Yes. And someone should tell her the sad news."

"You can tell her afterward. Watanabe-san is waiting."

I sighed. I knew it would be rude to argue at a time like this, so I dropped my head and followed her down the road.

My entire family walked down to Watanabe-san's house. Members from the NA joined us in the procession. In her window a black ribbon hung beneath her Japanese flag—in honor of her dead son and husband. A plaque with the characters for HOME OF HEROIC SPIRIT adorned her door. Watanabe-san greeted us with a stoic expression and bloodshot eyes. I had overheard at one of Aunt Kimiko's NA meetings that the government expected its citizens to act indifferent during public mourning—even if it was your son or husband who had been killed. All sacrifices were for the Emperor's honor. Grieving with emotion took place behind closed shoji doors. But I was still surprised that Watanabe-san could hide her sadness so well despite her great loss.

Watanabe-san bowed low to Papa and he bowed in return. Aunt Kimiko hugged her, and Sumiyo put her arm around her. We all walked in silence to the boatyard. We stopped at the train tracks even though very few trains came through to bring army supplies anymore. As expected, there were no trains this morning. Across the rails, I noticed that the army clothing and provisions depot that once bustled with military soldiers had the atmosphere of a ghost town. In fact, the only soldier there was the one who stood at attention in front of the dock.

When the lone soldier saw Watanabe-san, he bowed and handed her a small wooden box wrapped in white cloth.

Watanabe-san bowed in return and spoke her rehearsed line: "What a great honor to have a son die while serving the Emperor." We then began our walk home, again in silence.

I kept thinking that a tiny box held what was left of Jiro-san. I began to worry more about Akira-san. He had left three weeks ago to visit various islands in the Pacific so he could write about the battles for Papa's newspaper. Even though Akira-san was not a soldier and would not be fighting in the war, I knew it was still very dangerous for him to be near the front lines. I prayed that we would not have to make this trip someday for Akira-san's remains. My body shuddered and I wrapped my arms around my chest.

I was brought out of my thoughts by Papa's hand pulling me back so I didn't run into Sumiyo and Watanabe-san. Somehow, we were at the entrance to her home.

Watanabe-san did not speak immediately. It was like she didn't want to go inside. When she was alone she would only have her memories to comfort her. She turned and said, "Thank you very much for all your kindness." She bowed low to us.

My papa replied, "We are deeply sorry. Please let us know if there is anything you need."

Sumiyo and Aunt Kimiko each gave Watanabe-san a hug, and then she entered her home alone, holding the small wooden coffin against her chest.

We walked in silence. Only one thought occupied my mind. *How would I tell Machiko?*

CHAPTER SIXTEEN

*"INVEST IN JAPANESE WAR BONDS THROUGH
YOUR NEIGHBORHOOD ASSOCIATION."*

War poster

As we approached our house, I turned to Sumiyo and said, "I am going to see Machiko now. Someone has to tell her that Jiro-san is dead."

"Of course. I feel odd saying this given what we just witnessed, but we will be preparing for Oshagatsu. Your Aunt Kimiko and I will be addressing the nengajo postcards so they can be delivered tomorrow. Your Uncle Daichi's family will be arriving shortly and we will all be preparing the mochi. So, please do not stay at Machiko-san's too long." She squeezed my hand.

Papa kissed me good-bye as he was heading to the office to settle the year's bills so that the newspaper would have a fresh start on January first. I walked past my house and over to Machiko's. She opened the door after my first knock.

"Ohayo, Yuriko! Please, come in. I'm watching my younger brother while my mom is doing errands. Yuriko, what's wrong? Your face is so pale!"

I entered her house, trying to hide my sadness as best I could. Machiko and Papa were the two people who could always tell how I really felt just by looking at me, though.

"Maybe we should go to my room. My brother is sleeping in the living room and it looks like whatever this is, it's serious."

In her room, she sat on the tatami mat and patted the spot next to her. I continued to stand so she stood back up to face me.

"Oh, Machiko, I don't know any good way to say this, but this morning we went with Watanabe-san to receive the remains of Jiro-san at the boatyard."

Machiko's eyes widened as she put her hand to her mouth. "I hadn't heard that he was killed." Tears sprang to her eyes and she looked as if she might faint. I tugged at her hand so we could both sit on the tatami mat.

Machiko whispered, "It makes the war seem so real, doesn't it?"

"I guess no one is really safe during war."

"The other day I heard my father talking about a new bride," said Machiko in between sniffles. "Her husband was sent to fight after their wedding. She did not want her new husband to worry about *her* safety. She killed herself and in her note explained that she was doing this small act so her husband could fight with his whole heart for the Emperor." There was a catch in her voice. She wiped her eyes with a tissue.

Her words left me speechless. I couldn't help but wonder if Machiko would have done something like that if she would have been married to Jiro-san. A shiver went through me and I had to brush the thought aside. "I guess soldiers are not the only ones dying in this war." Machiko put her head on my shoulder and I hugged her.

"Yuriko, I know what my wish for the New Year will be. I wish that we can have peace. It has to come sooner or later, so why not this year?"

"Yes, that will be our wish when the temple bell rings at the shrine on New Year's morning," I agreed, and we smiled weakly at each other.

Wiping her cheeks and taking a deep breath, Machiko's face turned stoic and she said, "I have to sew on some labels for my mother. Would you like to help me?" She slid a box over from her closet in the corner of her room.

I picked up some labels. She put on her jazz record quietly in the background, and we attempted to erase the news from this morning with the lively notes of a swinging saxophone.

"I am home!" Machiko's mother called out.

I turned to Machiko, "I really should go home and help with preparations for the festival. I'll see you over the New Year break."

"Sayonara, and thank you for telling me the news about Jiro-san so I wouldn't hear it from someone else." Machiko hugged me. I didn't expect to be thanked for giving her such miserable news, but was glad she felt I helped her in some way.

I arrived home, kicked off my shoes, and was lured to the kitchen by the sweet and sour scent of sugar and vinegar in the norimaki rice balls. Sumiyo and Aunt Kimiko had been busy preparing meals for the New Year. We would need a large amount of food for us and the out-of-town relatives who visited once a year for the three-day New Year celebration. The only relatives from my mother's side were Aunt Kimiko and Genji. Sumiyo's sister and nieces lived in Sapporo and couldn't get away. However, Papa's one brother, Daichi-san, and his family lived three hours away. We only saw them at Oshagatsu or during summer holiday when we went to their guest cottage in the country. Although this year, because of the wedding, it wasn't too long between visits. From the chatter in the kitchen I could tell they were already here.

"Ton tsu ten ton . . ." Familiar voices sang the mochi cake song above the kitchen symphony of clanking utensils, plates, and pans.

"Ton." Sumiyo placed mochi, the sticky rice mixture, on the pedestal.

"Tsu." Uncle Daichi pounded the mochi with a large wooden mallet.

"Ten." Aunt Kimiko turned the flattened mochi right

before my uncle's mallet fell one more time.

As I walked into the kitchen they paused to greet me and then resumed their rhythmic pounding.

Once the sticky rice cakes were flattened, Aunt Emi, Uncle Daichi's wife, and I tore the cakes into small sections, coated them with cornstarch, and rolled them into balls. Genji helped my cousin, Naomi, place them into the black lacquer boxes for storage, where they would wait in preparation for the New Year soup.

As I finished singing the last line of the mochi cake song, a hand rested on my arm. I turned and saw our maid, Fumi-san.

"Yuriko-chan, please come look at the front door and tell me if the shimekazari is straight. We won't be able to stop the evil spirits from ruining our New Year if the decoration is not right." I laughed a little because Fumi-san was very superstitious.

"Yes, of course," I said, wiping leftover corn starch off my hands.

I had been the official decorator of our New Year's front door for as long as I could remember. I walked past the dining room on my way to the entrance. Papa was opening the heavy mahogany pocket doors so we would have one large living space for our New Year's celebration. After that, he and my uncle would add more leaves to the dining room table. We needed extra space because there would also be many local visitors stopping by to eat with us over the next few days.

I walked outside and looked at the door. Each year a new

shimekazari was made. Rope was twisted into the shape of a wreath, and then it was decorated with our samurai family crest, a fan, berries, and a small orange. I looked at the door from two different angles and then declared, "I think it needs more berries."

Fumi-san laughed. "You say that every year, Yuriko-chan!"

"Well, I like the look of berries."

My aunt called me from the kitchen. "Yuriko-chan, please help set out the holiday silk zabuton in the dining room."

I turned and went toward the side kitchen door. Fumi-san said, "Yuriko-chan, she asked you to help with the cushions in the dining room."

"I know, but I am thirsty." Fumi-san shook her head at me.

I shivered from the winter wind that blew through the door and into our hallway. I entered the steamy kitchen and asked one of the cooks for a cup of tea to warm me up. The tea kettle simmered on the stove all day this time of year. As I sipped from my cup, I heard Sumiyo directing Uncle Daichi to be careful setting up the kirinoki. I peered into the living room.

"Please be gentle. That antique stand has graced the Ishikawa's tokonoma for generations, and I cannot have it broken under my direction!"

Once Uncle Daichi delicately maneuvered the stand into place, I watched Sumiyo as she stacked two mochi cakes on it. The round cakes represented the sun and the moon, symbolizing good luck, harmony, and a long life. A green leaf and a dai-dai were placed on top. The small orange stood for the hope that one's family would carry on generation after generation. I flinched, knowing that for Watanabe-san, this would never happen.

I heard Aunt Kimiko's voice as she asked my stepmother, "Have you seen Yuriko-chan? She is supposed to help me."

I took that as my cue and left my empty teacup on the kitchen table.

"Here I am," I said as sweetly as possible.

Aunt Kimiko glared at me. It was too easy to annoy her. I removed the cushions from the box and set each one around the dining room table. I paused at the glass garden doors to admire the red and orange splash of color on the maple trees, which was reflected in the koi pond.

Papa came in from the garden and helped me finish preparing the dining room. "Joya, Akira-san will be home late tomorrow afternoon, just in time for Oshagatsu."

"Really? What a great surprise! I did not think we'd see him until after the New Year." I beamed.

"Yes, it is. We will all go to greet him at the train station. I am going to take my bath now. Please go and help your stepmother." He kissed the top of my head and retreated up the stairs.

Sumiyo asked if I could help Fumi-san bring the tea into the sunroom. She wanted to visit with my uncle and his family as this would be their first opportunity to get to know each other, since the wedding was such a busy day.

On the way to the kitchen I could hear Fumi-san and Genji singing the Oshagatsu song and I joined in: "Come, come quickly, New Year's Day."

CHAPTER SEVENTEEN

"In the Face of Warnings That War Situation More Severe, Let Us Greet the New Year With a Faith in Inevitable Victory."

Showa 20 January 1, Monday edition

The next day, at the train station, Akira-san waved to us from the platform. He was dressed in khaki pants and a khaki dress shirt. Through his smile I noticed that his face looked haggard and his cheeks were sunken. He had departed only one short month ago for a writing assignment, but already he looked much older than the day he left.

He bowed low as he greeted my papa and said, "It is good to see you again, sir."

"It is good to see you as well, Akira-san. Welcome home." Papa bowed in return.

Akira-san then turned to Aunt Kimiko, smiled, and

bowed. Aunt Kimiko bowed, and when she stood back up, I could see her face was flushed. Genji had been jumping up and down the entire time, but at least refrained from calling out to him until Papa and Aunt Kimiko had given him their greetings. Finally, Genji couldn't hold in his excitement any longer and he leaped up to hug his stepfather. Since Genji was a child, he was the one family member allowed to show such affection in public, and it made me smile a bit. At least he was able to express how we all felt.

On the ride home, Akira-san and Papa discussed news about how our family members were doing. Aunt Kimiko also talked about her increasingly important role with the NA. I wanted to know how the battles were going in the Pacific, but I knew that wouldn't be discussed in front of Genji or me. War matters should not concern children—at least that's what Papa often said.

We arrived home and Akira-san excused himself to take a bath and to put on fresh clothing. Aunt Kimiko, Sumiyo, and I went into the kitchen to retrieve the lacquered boxes of mochi cakes we had prepared yesterday.

Once Akira-san came back downstairs, we settled in the dining room, and the family New Year celebration began. I was about to have my first slurp of the yummy noodles in the special New Year soup when I heard the faint notes of a bamboo flute, a taiko drum, and a samisen in the distance. The noodles slipped off my chopsticks. The one Oshagatsu tradition I loathed, Shishi-mai, the lion dancers, was about to arrive at our door and ruin my supper.

Each Shishi-mai head was made of wood painted red with a shiny gold finish. It was worn by two people covered with green, red, and white fabric. The lion's eyes were a fiery red color and its mouth was wide open with golden teeth bared, as if ready to pounce and shred its prey. I knew there were people inside, but the lion masks had terrified me since I was very young.

Part of the New Year tradition is to have the lion "bite" your head to give you good luck throughout the year. When I was four Papa surprised me when he picked me up and brought my head to the lion's mouth. I screamed in sheer terror! I hated the loud noise of the drum. The blue markings on the lion's face along with its ghoulish long white mane frightened me. I had nightmares for days after.

"Joya, it's time you took part in this tradition again. Go out and stick your head into the lion's mouth," Papa said in a somewhat serious tone.

"No, thank you." I got up from my seat and backed slowly away from the table.

Papa clasped his hands behind his back and patiently waited to see if I would change my mind. When I did not, he said, "No need to be afraid of the Shishi-mai. If you put your head in the Shishi-mai's mouth, you will be protected."

My arms folded across my chest, I clamped my lips shut, and I moved my head side to side. "Ie, no, I do not like that tradition."

The music grew louder. The lion approached the open front door. My temples throbbed with each drumbeat.

I ran out of the room. I could hear laughter as I fled. Within minutes the music sounded farther away and Papa came to get me in my room.

"Joya, they are gone. Everything is fine. Come back and eat some the delicious toshikoshi soba Aunt Kimiko has prepared. Soon they will be ringing the temple bell." He hugged me. "I should have never surprised you with the lion when you were young. I did not mean to scare you from Shishi-mai for the rest of your life."

I took Papa's hand as the temple bell began striking. It rang out 108 times. Each toll of the bell was intended to symbolize the release of a sin or bad habit, giving a fresh start to the New Year. But with each *bong* I sat wishing, "Peace, peace, peace . . ."

CHAPTER EIGHTEEN

*"LOCAL SHIPYARDS PRODUCING
SIXTY SPECIAL SUBS DAILY."*

Showa 20 March 8 edition

I passed a bus stop while walking home from school and recognized the woman standing there as a local teahouse owner.
She also happened to be Yakamura-sensei's mother. Oh no!
What if she said something to me about being the reason for
her daughter's reassignment to another class? Maybe I could
cross the road before she saw me.

"Good afternoon, Yuriko-chan," she called out to me. Too
late!

"Good afternoon, Tanaka-san," I said as I bowed. My
cheeks burned and my heartbeat pulsed in my ears. I fought
the urge to run.

She looked at me and said, "Ah, Yuriko-chan, what a
beautiful young lady you are now. How Nishimoto-san would

love to see you. He must wonder about you! Not being allowed to see you for so long." Tanaka-san tilted her head and raised an eyebrow.

"What are you talking about? Who is Nishimoto-san?"

"Why he's your—oh, I am sorry, but I must catch the last bus," she said quickly.

She hurried up the bus's steps and the door closed behind her. I started to run after the bus as I yelled, "He is my what? Who is Nishimoto-san? Come back. Tell me!"

The black exhaust smoke made me cough, and I had to stop running. The bus disappeared down the street. I walked the remaining block home while catching my breath.

I did not go to Machiko's house like I normally would have after school. Instead, I went home, slammed the front door, and kicked off my shoes. Aunt Kimiko appeared and yelled, "I have told you before, do not slam the door!" She noticed my shoes. "Yuriko-chan, put your shoes away!"

I stood still, glaring at her. "Where is Papa?"

"I am the only one home right now. Pick up those shoes!"

My aunt was the last person I wanted to talk to, but if I didn't say something, I was going to burst.

"Who is Nishimoto-san?" I blurted out in one breath.

Aunt Kimiko's eyes widened as she turned away from me. Something was definitely wrong. She had never turned away from me before. I walked over and touched her shoulder. My hand trembled. I wanted her to talk to me, but for some reason I was also afraid.

Finally, my curiosity got the better of me and I said, "Look at me, Aunt Kimiko. Who is Nishimoto-san? Is that someone you know?"

Aunt Kimiko turned, looked directly at me, and said four words as expressionlessly as if she was telling me the weather: "He is your father."

●●●

My head spun as the floor seemed to move beneath me. I heard myself screaming, "No, no, no! You are lying!" as if it were another person besides me. Beads of perspiration formed on my forehead.

"Papa is my papa!" I yelled at her through the tears welling in my eyes. My throat felt like I was choking on sticky mochi.

Aunt Kimiko grabbed my shoulders. "Yuriko-chan, please sit down," she said, in a calm, measured voice.

I sat on a cushion on the tatami floor. I couldn't say anything else. I just looked up at Aunt Kimiko as she continued to speak. "Who mentioned his name to you?"

"Tanaka-san was at the bus stop. She said he must wonder about me because he had not been allowed to see me," I said, barely in a whisper.

"Tanaka-san is an osekkaina *and* Yakamura-sensei's mother. I knew this day would come, especially after the wedding."

My first instinct was to get up and run to my room, but I

was determined to show defiance for as long as I could. I narrowed my eyes and gave my aunt my best icy glare. "Tell me what this is all about."

Aunt Kimiko knelt opposite me, fixed her kimono by her feet, and after a long sigh began. "I was working at my father's company as a typist. I met Nishimoto-san there. He was one of my father's best journalists. I fell in love with him and brought shame to my family by becoming pregnant before I was married. It was made worse because it was with a man my father did not like. He had arranged for me to marry Akira back then. But I—"

"Wait, what does this have to do with me? You cannot mean you were pregnant with Genji. He is too young. You cannot mean . . . me? No, no, no." With each word I slapped my hand on the tatami mat. "You are lying! This cannot be true!" This was a nightmare. I wanted to wake up. Then I wanted to throw up.

Aunt Kimiko continued to speak in a calm voice. "When I told my father I was expecting a child, he, of course, was very angry with me. I did not honor my family by getting pregnant before being married. My mother intervened and calmed him down. The last thing he said to me before he banished me that night was that the child would be raised as his."

"You expect me to believe this story? What could I have possibly done to cause you to be so mean and to tell such a lie?" Tears were now streaming down my face.

"Shortly after you were born, my father followed through

on his threat and adopted you as his own. Having no other choice, I married Nishimoto-san. We had Genji, and a couple of years after that, we divorced. After the divorce, I was still afraid to come home. Uncle Daichi invited Genji and me to live with him. He strongly believed that my father should meet and accept his only grandson. Uncle Daichi visited him. They argued and Uncle Daichi reminded him that there is honor in forgiveness."

A memory flashed in my head and I mumbled, "It was more than just an argument. I remember that day."

"What are you saying?" Aunt Kimiko's eyes widened.

I focused on my hands folded on top of my lap as I spoke. "I woke up during the night and had to go to the bathroom. On my way down the hall, I heard furniture moving and some voices. One was Papa's. The whispering soon became shouting. I heard the sound of something falling. I peeked around the corner and was surprised to see Papa and Uncle Daichi rolling on the ground fighting. I had never seen Papa so angry. Papa—"

Aunt Kimiko interrupted, "They were actually fighting?"

"Papa had his brother pinned to the ground and a hand up ready to strike. He was looking into his brother's eyes. But instead of striking Uncle Daichi, Papa stood up, walked toward the door, and opened it. On the way out the door Uncle Daichi stated, 'There is honor in forgiveness.'"

I paused and thought, *It must be true. Papa is Aunt Kimiko's father. And not mine.* I shut my eyes tightly in an effort to escape this terrible moment of truth. But my tears escaped.

"Did your papa see you?"

"No, I hid in the shadows. Papa slowly straightened up the room, walked over to our Buddha shrine, and picked up the picture of Mama. It was the one time I ever saw him cry." I lifted my gaze and stared into Aunt Kimiko's eyes. "You and Genji moved in two days later."

Aunt Kimiko's hand lifted as if to caress my face but stopped short. Slowly she placed it back on her lap. For a brief second Aunt Kimiko's eye softened. In all the time she had lived here, pity was one look she never gave me. At that moment, I knew she was telling me the truth.

"Yuriko-chan, you must know deep down that I am not lying. Think back to the whispers and your koseki project. You do not think that Yakamura-sensei was fired because she was wrong?"

Fired? I thought she was simply transferred to another classroom because of the way she spoke to me. No wonder Tanaka-san said what she had. She must have been so angry with me for what I'd unknowingly done to Yakamura-sensei.

"I also remember you moving in and telling me you were my aunt. You lied to me—how could you do that? How could you give me up and lie to me all this time?" As I heard myself speak those words, I couldn't believe they were coming out of my mouth.

Aunt Kimiko's eyes started to water and her voice became high pitched. "I did what I had to do. I had shamed my family.

I had no choice!"

She now looked through me as if she were watching some scene play out in front of her.

"Yuriko-chan, you deserve to hear the truth from me. I know you will hate me, but I am no longer your mother. I did not raise you, and I do not expect anything in return. I expect you to keep treating me as if I were your aunt."

As she spoke, my anger toward her bubbled inside my veins and flowed like lava from a volcano. I stood, turned, and ran up the stairs to my room. She didn't call my name or come after me. Not that I expected that of her. I slid the shoji door shut and stomped to my night table.

I picked up the picture of Papa and me from when I was about five years old. All I could see was love in his eyes. Papa had kept this secret from me as well. My body shook and I sank down to my futon, I muffled my cry in my pillow. I wasn't sure if my tears were for me, for my papa, or for the fact that people outside my family, like my teacher and the woman at the teahouse, knew the truth before I did. Who else knew? Why didn't anyone tell me sooner?

• • •

I heard water running in the bathroom down the hall. It was dark in my room, and light peeked in through the shoji screen. I must have fallen asleep. Wait! Water—Papa was home! I had to talk to him before Aunt Kimiko did.

I knocked on the bathroom shoji door. "Papa, can I talk to you?" I said, trying to keep my voice from trembling.

"Joya, I will be out of the bath soon, and then we can talk."

"Papa, I know about Nishimoto-san," I blurted out.

I heard water slosh against the side of the tub. Suddenly the shoji door opened. Papa's yukata covered him as water dripped onto the floor. He walked right past me toward Aunt Kimiko's room, leaving behind puddles in the hallway.

He stopped, walked back to me, and lifted my chin so I could look at him as he said, "Joya, please wait for me in your room and we can talk, neh?"

I nodded my head, but as soon as he entered Aunt Kimiko's room, I tiptoed toward it. I was not going to miss my opportunity to hear this discussion. I expected to hear him shouting at her. Instead, it was more of a stern, controlled whisper. Aunt Kimiko's voice rose higher as she exclaimed, "She came to me. Tanaka-san said something to her. You know she is friends with his grandmother *and* Yakamura-sensei's mother. I did not see any other way. Yuriko is too persistent. She would not let it drop."

"She would have been told when I said she was ready to be told." Papa's voice bellowed, and I heard his pounding footsteps as he marched toward the door to Aunt Kimiko's room. I bolted into my room. It was wiser to stay there until he came to speak to me.

I had read the same sentence in my book five times but I could not stop wondering what Papa would say. I fantasized that he would tell me that Aunt Kimiko lied and she would be moving out immediately. However, I knew in my heart that she had not and that she would not be moving.

After what seemed an eternity, Papa knocked then slid back my door. He was dry and wore a different yukata. I inhaled the scent of his cologne hoping it would comfort me and swallowed the urge to cry. He looked miserable. He held out his hand as he said, "Yuriko-chan, come with me to the garden so we can talk."

I squeezed his hand. "Yes, Papa." I could not and would *never* call him anything else.

We entered the garden in silence and sat on the wrought iron bench in front of the koi pond. Papa exhaled and cleared his throat. But he didn't speak. Even though it was very warm outside, my body felt cold and clammy. I inhaled the sweet fragrance of the newly blossomed oleanders. It seemed fitting that they were in bloom because, like my Aunt Kimiko, they were beautiful on the outside, but toxic inside.

The silence was broken by the soft click-clacking of our garden's bamboo trees, swaying in the evening breeze. Normally this sound was soothing, calming. But that night it sounded like the ticking of a bomb before it exploded.

Papa exhaled again and finally spoke. "Joya, I know the news you heard today must be a shock to you. I am going to be honest and say that I had no intention of you hearing of this—of Nishimoto-san—until much later."

Papa practically spat out his name. In that moment, I

wanted to forget this ever happened. But I had to reply with something. "I think I understand, Papa. I needed to ask because I was confused. But I did not mean to cause any trouble."

"Joya, I am not mad at you at all. That woman should not have said anything to you. I will admit to you that once Kimiko-san married Akira-san, I gave serious thought about you calling Akira-san 'father' *after* I told you about this situation. He technically is your stepfather now and will be alive longer than I will. Perhaps, you might think about that."

I raised my eyebrows then tried to say something. But no words came out. Papa hugged me close and said, "I love you very much, and nothing will *ever* change that. Do you understand?"

But I couldn't understand. All I wanted was to end this conversation and to let my papa know I loved him. So I took a deep breath and replied, "I know you love me and I love you. That is all that matters to me right now. It is all I want."

That, and for life to go back to the way it was mere hours ago, when I was Papa's daughter and everything was normal.

CHAPTER NINETEEN

*"No Matter What Sort of Air Raid Comes,
This Neighborhood Association
Will Be Safe."*

Neighborhood Association poster

I tossed and turned all night. Every time I closed my eyes I saw Aunt Kimiko telling me about Nishimoto-san, followed by my teacher's voice saying, 'That is not right.' Sunlight peeked under the blackout curtains. I decided I might as well get up and have breakfast. I sat up and remembered that we didn't have school today. And the Shintenchi movie theater would be showing a movie here in our house for our neighborhood this afternoon. Maybe that would take my mind off this whole mess. Plus, Machiko would be here and I had to tell her what I'd just learned.

I dressed and went into the kitchen for breakfast. Fumi-san had the radio's "Home War Hour" show on. It was later in the morning than I had thought, since the radio program ended at 10:30 a.m.

"That is our program for March 9, 1945. We end this hour with the winning slogan from NHK Radio's monthly slogan contest: without a strong, stable family there can be no victory." I couldn't help but think if that was truly the case, then Japan was doomed, given my family.

"Ohayo Yuriko-chan." Fumi-san shut off the radio and brought me some miso soup.

"Ohayo, Fumi-san."

"Today is the big movie day. The movie theater employees are here now. They brought in this large white screen into the dining room. Wait until you see it! All the doors had to be slid open to make one enormous room. Your papa's generosity to people by bringing the movies to your house so the entire neighborhood can see and enjoy it is unmatched. Especially during the war, since spending money at a theater is certainly not a luxury most families can afford."

Her enthusiasm brightened my mood a little. "Yes, it should be fun to watch a movie right here at home, with our neighbors."

Papa planned to show a Three Stooges movie. The Three Stooges were American actors and the movie was about three brothers who were not very smart, who tended to be very mean to each other, and who loved to poke each other in the eyes. I didn't find them that funny, but Papa loved their movies and laughed all the way through them. Tears filled his eyes and his broad shoulders shook up and down. I enjoyed seeing him so happy, so I grew to be fond of the silly movies, too.

I finished my soup and brought the bowl to the sink. "Thank you Fumi-san. I am going to get my seat in the dining room." I left the kitchen just as our neighbors were arriving. The front rooms looked so large with all the shoji doors pushed aside, but as the people kept coming in I began to wonder if we would all fit.

Machiko arrived with her little brothers shortly before we started the movie. I sat in the front row between Machiko and Papa. I had never seen so many people in our room. The crowd spilled out into the front hall.

"Yuriko, you should see all the shoes outside your house. There must be fifty pairs making a path all the way to the street!" Machiko exclaimed.

"I know. It's exciting." I tried to make my voice sound normal, but I was still reeling from the news about Papa and Aunt Kimiko, and I felt my voice falter a bit.

"Yuriko, what's wrong? You don't sound like yourself." She leaned in and put her hand on mine.

I should have known it would be difficult to hide anything from my best friend. I wanted to tell her about my family secret, but I could never do that in front of Papa and with all these people in our home.

"It is nothing to worry about. I'll tell you about it later," I said, trying to make my voice sound normal.

Machiko raised an eyebrow, and I knew she didn't believe me. Luckily, I didn't have to try to convince her further because the movie theater owner clapped his hands and announced, "Attention, attention! The movie is about to begin."

The murmuring stopped as the film started to roll. First there was the obligatory newsreel. In the first few minutes, we watched the rest of Asia cheering the Japanese army's victory march after winning some recent invasion, or, at least, that was the impression given in the clip. The announcer stated that the Emperor's picture was about to be shown. All heads bowed out of respect to our Emperor. Then the Three Stooges film finally began.

Many people thought my papa was always serious, but that night Papa showed them he had a sense of humor, too. It made everyone else laugh that much harder as he howled at the antics on screen.

When the credits rolled, everyone clapped. Papa went to the front door to thank the people for coming. They thanked him in return. For a couple of hours I had forgotten about the war and my family secret. It was wonderful to feel joyful again.

Before Machiko left she pulled me aside. "Yuriko-chan, I know that something is wrong. Can you come over tomorrow? I promised to bring my brothers straight home after the movie, so I have to leave now. But I also have something to tell you."

"Oh really? Okay, I will visit tomorrow afternoon.

Sayonara!" I said, beaming her a big smile.

"Sayonara! Thank you. We had so much fun." Machiko hugged me and gathered her brothers for the walk home.

This was perfect. Now I'd have time to think about the best way to tell her my secret. If anyone could help me make sense of it, it was Machiko.

I helped Sumiyo and Aunt Kimiko put away the extra chairs. After Papa paid the movie theater owner, he went into the newspaper office. I spent the rest of the day reading and most of the night staring at the ceiling wondering what Machiko wanted to tell me. It couldn't possibly be as complicated as what I had to tell her.

CHAPTER TWENTY

"Any Enemy Landing Will Be Smashed."

Showa 20 March 10 edition

"*Now* will you tell me what happened yesterday that upset you so much? I can tell by your face that it's something serious," Machiko said as we huddled on her bedroom floor.

"I don't know where to start." I cleared my throat and began to wipe my sweaty palms on my monpe pants.

"Please, just tell me," Machiko pleaded. "You can trust me."

I rubbed my palms together and took a deep breath before starting, "I ran into this woman who owns one of the teahouses. She said the oddest thing to me." I paused, trying to think how to tell her about the rest of the conversation.

Machiko moved her hand in a forward motion and spoke in an urgent tone, "All right, what did she say?"

I couldn't get the words out. I ran my fingers through my bangs.

"Yuriko, please tell me. What did she say to you?" Machiko pleaded. She pulled my hand away from my hair and held it in hers.

"She said—" I stopped. It still seemed so impossible to me. I was afraid to say it out loud to someone. That would mean I had accepted it as the truth. But finally, after sighing deeply, I continued. "She said that Nishimoto-san would love to see the young lady I have become."

"Well, that doesn't sound so bad. Is Nishimoto-san a friend of your family, then?" Machiko asked, giving me a very confused look.

"Then she said how he had not been *allowed* to see me. And when I asked her who he was, she stopped herself from answering and got on the bus." I pulled my hand away from hers, stood up, and began to pace, tapping my fists on my legs.

"Is he a relative, then?" She looked up at me.

"No. Actually, he . . ." I bit my lip then said, ". . . he is my father." I said it so fast it came out as one long word instead of a sentence.

Machiko's eyes and mouth opened wide as she stared at me. "Your father?" She covered her mouth with both hands and stood up.

"Unbelievable, neh?"

Machiko shook her head. "That makes no sense, Yuriko. You have a father. This can't be true. She could just be spreading gossip. She—"

"But Machiko, she is also Yakamura-sensei's mother. I got her daughter fired!"

"*You* got her fired?"

"Well, not me exactly. My papa did. But it was because of me telling him that my teacher said 'that is not right' in regard to my koseki." I took a deep breath and sighed.

I continued, "So, after she boarded the bus, I walked home to get answers. I knew my papa would have an explanation, but he wasn't there. I had no one to ask except Aunt Kimiko." I was not about to call her mother—not today, not ever. "She told me that Nishimoto-san was my . . . my real father."

I looked at Machiko. She had tears in her eyes as I did in mine. "She said it with so much conviction. And she looked sorry for me. That frightened me the most. In my head I knew she wasn't lying, but my heart fought with her."

"But, if your papa isn't your papa, who is your mother then?"

I locked eyes with her and shook my head slowly from side to side. "You won't believe this. The person I like the least . . ."

"Oh, no, no—*not* Kimiko-san. She cannot be your . . ."

I nodded my head, "Yes, *she* is my birth mother. It's a nightmare come true. Aunt Kimiko said that she was in love with Nishimoto-san and shamed the family when she got pregnant with me before marrying him. Papa, who I guess is really my grandfather, said he would raise the child—me. So Aunt Kimiko gave me up. She married my birth father and they had that monkey, Genji. When she got divorced, she moved in with us."

Machiko stepped closer and put her arms around me. Tears streamed down my cheeks as I hugged her back. She leaned back, put her hands on my shoulders, and said, "I wish I had something good to say to make you feel better about this. But I have nothing. This must be so hard for you!"

I wiped away my tears with my hand and said, "There isn't much that can be said to make the truth any easier. The one good thing is that Aunt Kimiko doesn't expect to be treated as my mother. At least we both finally agree on something."

"What did your papa say about this?"

"He was angry. But he didn't lie to me. He told me it was the truth and that he had planned to tell me when I was older. He did say one thing that bothered me, though. He thought I should eventually call Akira-san father, since he is technically my stepfather now."

"What about this Nishimoto-san? Do you want to meet him?"

"Machiko, I don't know where he is and I don't care. He must have agreed to give me up as well. I have a papa and now a stepfather, too. I *don't* need any more parents." I gave a weak smile. I felt relieved, having gotten the secret off my chest, but now I had said all that I wanted to say about my family. And then I remembered that Machiko had something she wanted to tell me.

"I am sorry, Machiko. You asked me here to tell me something and I've just been talking about me. Please, tell me your news."

"Oh, it's not important," she said with a wave of her hand.

"Of course it is. Please tell me. I'd rather not think about myself any longer."

"Well, it doesn't seem so awful now after your news, but I can't go back to school tomorrow."

"Why not?"

"I received notice that I am to report to the Hiroshima airplane factory instead."

My mouth dropped almost to the floor and my eyes opened as wide as possible. "What do you mean, you have to go to the factory? What will you be doing there? And for how long?" I would have rather run ten races than work in a factory for ten minutes.

"I don't know yet. I guess I'll find out once I'm there," she said with a small shrug.

"Will you have to live there?" I held my breath waiting for her reply and thought to myself, *What if they don't have enough food? What if the girls are mean? What if the bosses are mean?*

"No, not every night. There are two shifts. We'll alternate every other week. The first shift is from eight in the morning to three in the afternoon. I can come home after that. But I'll have to stay overnight and come home in the morning on the second shift from three in the afternoon to eleven at night. I'm not looking forward to that."

I could tell Machiko was nervous because she pushed a

lock of hair behind her ear, which she only did when she was unsure about something. I put my arm around her shoulder and said, "I'm so sorry and I understand why you'd be nervous. I would not be looking forward to that either. It doesn't sound like a fun way to spend the evening. But, I'm sure there will be some other nice girls there, too. That will help the time go faster."

In my mind, all I could think of was how much I would miss my papa if I had to go to a factory and stay overnight—not to mention, how much I would miss seeing Machiko after school on the weeks when she worked the second shift. I had never gone more than a day without speaking to her since we'd become friends.

"I am nervous for you, though," I said. As soon as that came out of my mouth, I wanted to take it back.

"I'm just hoping that it isn't too dangerous or difficult of work. My father has told me some horrible stories about girls who worked such long hours at run-down factories."

"I've heard those stories, too, Machiko. But that won't happen while you're there." I tried to sound hopeful, but I had knots in my stomach.

"You're probably right." Machiko paused and her eyes lit up. "We should talk about something happier, though. The Cherry Blossom Festival is coming up. Remember last year's celebration? We had so much fun together."

The unexpected sound of the shoji door being slid open made us both jump. Machiko's mother entered. She looked very pale and was sniffling. Her voice wavered as she told us, "Tokyo was bombed last night by the Americans. Not just regular bombs. These bombs caused huge windblown fires and most of Tokyo has burned to the ground."

CHAPTER TWENTY-ONE

*"WE ARE ONE HUNDRED MILLION PEOPLE,
ONE SPIRIT."*

NHK Radio slogan

We were in shock. Normally adults would not tell us news about the war. But this had clearly shaken Machiko's mother.

Machiko and I stood in silence, our mouths hanging open. If our divine Emperor's home city was bombed, any city in the whole of Japan could be in danger.

Machiko finally asked, "Do you think America will drop firebombs on all of the cities in Japan?"

Machiko's mother took out a tissue from her pocket and wiped tears from her cheeks. "If they do, most of the buildings in town will burn just as quickly as Tokyo's. You should go home now, Yuriko-chan. It's getting late."

Then she came over and gave me a big hug, which was unlike her. I squeezed her back.

I then hugged Machiko, said, "Sayonara," and left. I had forgotten all about Machiko going to the factory the next day. I had even forgotten to ask her to call me when she got home.

I entered our home through the front door. Usually, Aunt Kimiko and Sumiyo would be chatting in the dining room and Genji would be running around the house making lots of noise. But tonight no one was in the dining room. It was quiet inside except for Papa and Akira-san's voices coming from behind the closed door of Papa's study. I walked in the direction of the voices. I raised my hand to knock on the door, but the irritated tone in Papa's voice made me stop short. Instead, I placed my ear quietly to the shoji door and listened.

"I am a reporter. I write news. I started this company because I wanted people to be informed. I should be able to print the news without going through government censure committees." Papa's voice was booming and then I heard the sound of what had to be Papa's hand hitting the desk. I flinched.

"I completely understand. But the government will halt the delivery of our paper and ink supplies if we do not comply. Some editors have even been arrested for resisting this rule," Akira-san replied.

Arrested? Could Papa be arrested? What would happen to him—or to me? I swallowed the nausea that rose in my throat.

"I am aware of that. That is precisely why I hired an extra editor as a precaution." Papa sighed and continued, "However, I am aware that I cannot fight the government agencies. As much as I don't want to, we will continue to send our news through the censure committee. But I *refuse* to print any false victories in our paper. The misinformation we received and reported of Japan's latest victory in the Pacific was an embarrassment. If I have to report censored news, it will at least be truthful."

"Yes, of course," Akira-san agreed.

A prickling sensation traveled up and down my arms. I hadn't realized that we had actually lost that battle. *Do other countries lie about victories? Was that why Papa had mentioned the possibility of Japan losing the war?* My thoughts were interrupted by Papa's voice again.

"Akira-san, I have an important matter I wish to discuss." Papa spoke softer now and no longer sounded disgruntled. I pressed my ear closer to the door to hear him better. He cleared his throat and continued, "Now that you are married to Kimiko, you can officially be considered Yuriko-chan's stepfather. She has found out about"—he paused—"about her birth father."

I covered my mouth to muffle the involuntary gasp that escaped my lips.

"Ishikawa-san, that is not necessary. I do not want to step in—"

"I appreciate your respect, but this is how it will be now." I thought I heard his voice falter at the end of the sentence.

"Of course. I greatly appreciate your confidence in my role."

I pulled back a bit from the door, completely in shock. I didn't think Papa would really make good on his promise the other day in the garden—about Akira-san taking over the role of my father. I could never call anyone else Papa! A tear escaped my right eye as a lump grew at the back of my throat.

I heard a click of a knob, followed by some static, and soon an announcer's voice: *"At fifteen minutes past midnight on March tenth Tokyo was hit with a new kind of bomb, an incendiary, called a firebomb. The windy weather assisted the enemy's attack to spread the fire using the wooden buildings as kindling."*

The "Dawn to Sea" march played, ending the announcement, and I lost my footing. I fell toward the study door. I attempted to make it sound as if I were knocking instead of tumbling into the door while eavesdropping.

"Who is it?" Papa asked.

"It is me, Papa." I focused on pronouncing each word because I was afraid that any shakiness in my voice might give away the fact that I had heard their whole conversation.

"Come in, Joya."

I slid the door open and walked into the room. I expected Papa and Akira-san to admonish me for listening to their conversation. But if they suspected, they hid it from their expressions and said nothing.

"Did you hear the news about Tokyo?" Akira-san asked.

"Yes. I came home after Machiko's mother told us about it. When I entered the house, I heard the radio announcer, too." I was telling the truth, just not all of it. "Is the whole city destroyed?"

"We don't know how many people have been killed. However, the mayor of Hiroshima has decided that we must prepare for a similar attack and knock down all of our wooden buildings in the center of town. Hiroshima will not be burned like Tokyo," Papa answered.

"Do you really think they will bomb our city?" I asked, a quiver to my voice.

"Anything is possible in war." As Papa said this, my stomach swarmed with butterflies. I ran to him and welcomed his embrace.

"Papa, are we all going to be all right?" I squeezed tighter. I swear all one hundred million hearts from the radio slogan were beating in my chest. *Will fire be raining down on us soon? Maybe we should just live in the bomb shelters? But how is that really living?*

He hugged me close and then stepped back. He looked at me and said, "I will keep you safe."

Akira-san added, "Our family's safety is our main concern." He glanced at Papa. "But now you should get ready for bed. It is late."

I nodded and gave him a hug as well. When I got to the door, I turned and asked, "Papa, do you think we will have school tomorrow?"

I noticed that both he and Akira-san looked up to answer. I did not know what made me feel worse—the fear that this new firebomb could be dropped on Hiroshima next or the tugging of my heart as both men responded to "Papa." Akira-san looked down at his papers, his cheeks burning red.

Papa replied, "Yes, Joya. Good night."

"Good night, Papa." I kept my eyes on the floor, not wanting to hurt either one of them.

Everything was so confusing. Who was I supposed to call Papa now?

CHAPTER TWENTY-TWO

"You Will Be Defeating America With These Arms. Achieve Your Quota!"

Showa 20 March 27, Poster at airplane factory

Within a few weeks of the attack on Tokyo, Akira-san left for the Philippines to report on the battles in the Pacific. Spring had finally arrived, regardless of the war or bombings. As the days warmed and the birds sang more frequently, we prepared to welcome in the new season with the annual Cherry Blossom Festival.

"Yuriko-chan, will you help me pack for the picnic later this morning?" Sumiyo asked as I walked past her room.

"Yes, Sumiyo. I am going to Machiko's, but will not be long." Today was my first chance to catch up with Machiko since she started working at the plane factory. Her adjustment to her mixed up hours left her exhausted and she had little time to visit. But today she had off for the festival.

"Very well. Please let me know once you return," Sumiyo said.

I put on my shoes and went across the street. Machiko came out to the front door. "Yuriko, so wonderful to see you! It has been so long, neh?" She gave me a hug.

"Yes, too long! You must tell me everything. How is work? What do you have to do? How are the other girls at the factory?"

Machiko stepped back and put her hand up. "Okay, okay, let's go inside and I will tell you all about it. Although, it's not that exciting."

We went up to her room and I noticed a uniform hanging from the doorframe. "Is that yours for the plane factory?" I asked as I picked up and fingered the white kamikaze headband with the rising sun. My stomach tightened. These were the headbands worn by the soldiers who crashed into the enemy on purpose, knowing they would die for the Emperor.

"Yes, fashionable, neh? The navy blazer I wore to school, my monpe pants, and a white shirt. We must wear our student corps identification as well as our emergency supply satchel at all times. I'll be so happy to put on a kimono today because it will be a nice change."

I dropped the headband and turned to face her. "But what do you have to do at the factory all day?"

She sat on the tatami mat and I joined her. "Our nine-hour shifts don't include time to eat. I try to eat a big breakfast if I am going in for the day shift or a larger lunch if I am doing the night shift."

"Nine hours? That's a long time to do anything but sleep!" We both laughed.

"Well, we certainly don't sleep. We stand the entire time. As apprentices, we spend most of the shift watching and learning from the veteran workers. But sometimes they are too busy to show us and we just stand there. We can't read or eat to pass the time. Just watch them work. Such a waste and I get so bored. How are we helping the country fight the war by just standing there?"

"That's horrible! What are you learning to do?"

"I'm assigned to the lathe department. First, one department cuts a piece of steel into a rough shape of some engine part. Then it comes to my department. The lathe is this large bulky machine. We insert steel cylinders into it and there is a blade that cuts it to a certain measurement. Once the machine is moving, we have to be careful not to get hit with the pieces of metal that are shaved off. They are very hot and some girls have burns to prove it. When we complete our job, it goes to a finishing department. There, they measure it for accuracy."

I could only stare at her, trying to comprehend what this all would look like.

Machiko smiled and said, "I know. It is like learning another language. I'm still not exactly sure what to do."

"How horrible. Oh, Machiko, I am so sorry you have to do this."

"Well, the group of girls I'm with is very nice. When I work the day shift and sleep at home, it's not so bad. But when I have to stay the night, it's bad. They serve miso broth and a spoonful of rice to us. We only have these little thin blue sleeping mats. The dorms have no heat, so we freeze. I don't drink much water because I do *not* want to use the disgusting outside bathroom. And if there is an air raid alert, we don't sleep much. There was actually one night we didn't even bother moving to the air raid shelter during the alert. If a bomb was going to be dropped, we were too exhausted to care!"

"Oh. I don't know what to say."

"I know. I'm getting used to going to the factory now, though. But to be honest with you . . ." She looked out the window and sat back down. "I don't think there are actually any planes being manufactured. The other day I overheard one of the supervisors say that it didn't matter what we produced because there is no longer any fuel. In fact, some boys' jobs were to extract pinesap to see if could be used as fuel! Pinesap! For goodness sake, how do you win a war with pinesap?" She raised both hands and shook her head.

The thought that Japan would win the war became harder to believe with each story I heard. First, Papa's concern, now what Machiko overheard. I wiped my sweaty palms on my monpe pants. "I'm worried, Machiko."

"So am I. The Emperor is divine, though, and the gods saved Japan from an invasion long ago, so we must be hopeful."

I couldn't tell if Machiko believed what she was saying, but I so badly wanted it to be more than just folklore. "If you're still hopeful then I will remain hopeful."

Machiko smiled and said, "We have the Sakura Hanami later today and *that* will be fun!"

"Yes, my favorite festival! Even if I do have to wear a kimono. But I really should get back to help. I promised Sumiyo."

"I'm so glad you stopped over. I have been wanting to tell you all about my job, but never had the time." We stood and she gave me a quick hug. "See you under the cherry tree in a little while."

"Yes, see you soon." As I crossed the street I kept picturing poor Machiko in the cold, with little to eat, standing all day, and maybe doing it all for nothing. My thoughts didn't last long because the front door opened and Aunt Kimiko yelled, "There you are! Aren't you supposed to help Sumiyo?"

"Yes, but she knew I was at Machiko's."

"Well, I will tell her you're home."

I went into the kitchen, grabbed a pear, and saw Sumiyo coming down the stairs. "I am ready to help, Sumiyo."

"Wonderful. How is Machiko-chan doing with her work at the factory?"

"She spends a lot of time standing, operating clunky machinery, and it sounds awful." I left out Machiko's thought about her work probably not making a difference at all.

"She is a brave young woman. I will let you know when I need you."

"I will be reading in the study until then," I replied.

Sumiyo went toward the dining room. I walked into the study and headed toward my favorite chair. I passed Papa's desk and spied an airmail envelope with an opened letter next to it. I glanced to see who it was for. It was from Akira-san and was addressed to Aunt Kimiko. I knew it wasn't meant for me to read, but I couldn't resist. Besides, if Aunt Kimiko wanted to keep the letter's contents private, she shouldn't have left it out for anyone to see.

I peeked out the doorway to be sure no one was nearby, and then closed the study door. I ran on my tiptoes back to the desk, picked up the letter, and began to read. The first few lines were asking about her and the family. He spoke of missing us. But the next paragraph caught my attention:

Kimiko-san, the battles fought in the Pacific Islands have been the hardest for our troops. I cannot state much more than that. However, please keep your promise to me. If there is a land invasion and battle with the enemy, you will do as we discussed prior to my leaving. I know you have the inner strength to commit gyokusai. It is the only way I believe you and your family will be safe from enemy harm.

"Gyokusai—suicide?" I whispered to myself as the letter fell from my hand. The room seemed to spin for a moment. The last two sentences could have been taken straight out of an old samurai story.

"Yuriko-chan, I could use your help, please," Sumiyo called from outside the door. I jumped, grabbed the letter, placed it in its original position on the desk, and ran to my favorite chair. No sooner did I open my book than Sumiyo slid the door open. My heart fluttered against my chest as I inhaled deeply in an attempt to regain a semblance of calm.

"I am ready to help, Sumiyo." I paused as if finishing a sentence in the book before putting it down. As we left the room I gave a furtive glance at the shocking letter lying on the desk.

"I am so happy that we will be celebrating the cherry blossoms tomorrow as a family," Sumiyo said.

"Yes, I am, too. It's my favorite time of year, even if I have to wear a kimono." I clasped my hands and walked in exaggerated dainty steps to mimic a geisha. I hoped that if I did something funny, the ensuing laughter would mask my nerves. It seemed to work, because Sumiyo laughed with me and I felt a little better.

I spied Aunt Kimiko and the maid at the counter packing chicken teriyaki into the lacquered boxes for our picnic the next day. Kimiko turned the radio on for the hourly news broadcast and we heard the end of an announcement, "*. . . in Okinawa. I repeat: the Americans have stormed the Okinawan islet of Zamami. Two hundred women and children committed suicide to avoid capture and punishment from the Americans.*"

My stomach leapt to my throat. I had to swallow my gag reflex. I think we were stunned into silence by the announcement. Sumiyo cried out and covered her mouth as she shut off the radio. My thoughts immediately went to Akira-san's letter. *Was the enemy so horrible that being dead was better than being captured?* I looked around the room and tried to picture all of us doing what the Okinawan women and children had done. *Would we be brave enough to watch each other do that? Would I be brave enough to go through with it myself?* Just the thought of this made my stomach churn. Tears began to trickle down my cheeks. Were we crying for these strangers or simply out of fear for our own fate? I heard Genji's footsteps kicking at the stones in the garden. He was headed for the kitchen door. Aunt Kimiko, Fumi-san, and Sumiyo immediately reached for a towel and wiped their faces.

"Yuriko-chan, wipe those tears. I don't want Genji to know about this. He's too young," Aunt Kimiko said as she handed me a towel. When Genji got to the door, we were back to packing the lacquer boxes as if nothing had happened. Sumiyo began to hum a song that I'd noticed she often did when she wanted to hide something.

"I'm hungry, Mama." Genji ran inside and hugged his mother. As Aunt Kimiko turned to make him some soba noodles, I noticed that Genji had left muddy handprints on her back. Playing in the dirt was his only concern. I wondered how much longer he would be able to hold on to that innocence. There certainly was none left for me.

• • •

Sumiyo knocked on the shoji door to the dressing room and said, "Yuriko-chan, please come down and help me gather the large blankets for our picnic."

"Yes, Sumiyo, as soon as I adjust my obi."

"I thought Fumi-san helped you with that earlier?" Sumiyo peeked into the room. She looked stunning in her beautiful silk kimono from last year's celebration.

"She said I had to learn to tie it on my own," I said, letting out a frustrated sigh.

"Ah, I see," Sumiyo said. I managed to attach the obi, but it was crooked. Its cherry blossom design looked as if the tree branch was bent over in a monsoon. But it would have to do.

I entered the living room, and Papa handed me a blanket and a small basket. I looked inside and was happy to see I was holding the container with my favorite dessert, hanami dango—sweet rice cakes. The white, green, and pink colors stacked on the skewer looked like a mini cherry blossom tree.

"Are you sure you do not want to come with us, Papa?" I asked, giving his arm a gentle squeeze.

"Yes, Joya. I have work to do, but I will have the dining room prepared for the celebration when you return." He kissed me on the forehead, and then I followed the others into the car.

We drove about forty minutes to Hijiyama Park. Once we arrived, I picked up the blanket and small picnic basket. Children in their kimonos ran up and down the winding paths, pointing at the beautiful blossoms as their parents followed the trails of laughter to catch up with them. The paths were usually lined with paper luminaries so the blossoms' beauty could be enjoyed even after sunset. But the fear of nighttime bombings snuffed them out.

We managed to find a picnic spot right under a beautiful cherry tree in full bloom. Petals of light and dark pink rippled with white hung on the branches as if they themselves were delicate lanterns.

"I can see the tall buildings in downtown Hiroshima from here. In fact, I can see all the way to Hiroshima Bay!" I exclaimed.

"Yes, the view is almost as beautiful as all the cherry blossoms, neh?" Sumiyo replied.

As soon as we had set down our things, Machiko and her family joined us. They added their blanket next to ours. We began to unpack all of the delicious food that we would share for hanami.

"Yuriko, the cherry blossoms seem pinker than usual. Do you think so?" Machiko asked as she picked up norimaki with her chopsticks.

"Yes, they are breathtaking. It seems like there are more people here this year, too," I said as I stole teriyaki from Genji's plate while he looked up at the blossoms.

"I think we need to enjoy the beauty more this year since there is so much ugliness with the war. At the factory so many families have lost fathers, brothers, or both. For some the factory is their home now." Machiko frowned.

"That's awful. I'm sure a factory could never feel like a home." I took a bite of my favorite sweet rice cake. "We are both very lucky to have our families."

"And each other!" we added in unison.

Children gathered in the grassy area not covered by picnic blankets. Genji tapped me on my shoulder. "Yuriko, don't forget we are going to dance and sing, too, later on. You promised."

"Yes, I know." I sighed. I was so happy to be out enjoying the cherry blossoms that I was willing to keep my promise to annoying Genji just this once.

"Yuriko, my younger brothers want to sing and dance, too! We can all dance together," Machiko said between bites of teriyaki.

"That will be more fun than Genji and me dancing alone." I laughed.

"I wouldn't let you do it without me." Machiko smiled as she bumped against my shoulder.

The sun shone through the clouds and warmed my face. I looked around and saw people in boats rowing out to enjoy the view from the river. A breeze shook the cherry blossom branches, making the petals dance.

"Time to sing, Yuriko-chan!" Genji interrupted my thoughts.

I stood with Machiko and her brothers, and we all formed a circle. Genji took my right hand and Machiko was on my left. We began to run in a circle. We slowed down and began to clap while we sang the ancient song, "Cherry blossoms, cherry blossoms, on meadow, hill, and dale, as far as you can see, is it mist or clouds . . ."

Once our dance finished, we sat again on the blanket to watch the sunset. The purple and pinks of the sky made the perfect backdrop for the blossoms. A magical deep purple glow painted the sky. I wanted to hold this memory in my heart forever.

Finally, we packed up our belongings and drove back to the house. The dining room doors were opened and the lanterns were lit. When we entered the dining room, the sight of the beautiful cherry blossoms in our own garden took my breath away. Papa invited us to sit in one of the many chairs set up along our antique hinoki cypress table. Once we were all seated, Papa raised his glass and said, "Cherry blossoms are like life itself—so beautiful, yet so fragile that they bloom only a short time. A toast to my family and to enjoying our time together. Kanpai!"

We all replied with a joyful, "Kanpai!"

As I sipped my plum juice, I glanced down and noticed the little scuff marks that my geta sandals had made on the table when I was only four. Papa had placed me on the tabletop to entertain some guests by singing and dancing to the cherry blossom song.

"Yuriko-chan, did you hear me?" Genji asked.

"What? No, I'm sorry—what did you say?" I shook my head, coming out of my daydream.

"I asked if you were really allowed to dance on top of this table."

"Yes, Genji. I danced and sang on this table once."

"I'm jealous. You were so lucky."

"Yes, I was." I looked around the room at their happy faces, realizing that even though there is so much uncertainty and fear, joyful, happy moments still existed. And I smiled.

CHAPTER TWENTY-THREE

"THE JAPANESE ENACT A MAJOR OFFENSIVE IN THE SOUTH IN OKINAWA."

Showa 20 May 6, NHK Radio

"I think that you and the rest of the family should go to the country house for a few weeks," Papa announced the next morning while we were eating our breakfast.

"Why? I do not like it there, especially without you," I said, sticking out my bottom lip in a bit of a pout.

"It is for your safety in case of a firebomb being dropped here. Keeping you safe is my main concern. You know that I need to stay here to continue the newspaper."

"But—"

"No arguments, Joya. You are going. The decision has been made." He kissed the top of my head and turned me toward my bedroom. "Go pack."

I trudged to my room and found that the maid had already

started packing my suitcase. I was soon packed and ushered out the door and into the car. Papa waved good-bye to us at the train station and I was stuck next to my monkey cousin—I still could not think of him as my brother. I closed my eyes, trying to shut off my mind from everything that was bothering me.

"Yuriko-chan, are you awake? I am bored. Will you read to me?" Genji said, poking me with his index finger.

I closed my eyes tighter and deepened my breathing. Soon I heard Genji's box of crayons spill out onto the little table in front of us and I knew I had won this small battle for the time being.

•••

Suddenly, my body lurched forward and I banged my head against the seat in front of me. The train had reached the Bingo Tokaichi station. I must have fallen asleep, because I could see Papa's family waving to us from the platform.

"Yuriko-chan, we're here! We're here!" Genji poked me in the arm as he yelled directly into my ear.

"Yes, I can see that. Now, stop touching me and find your mother." I narrowed my eyes and gave him my best scowl.

He left to go find Aunt Kimiko. I grabbed my bag from under the seat with a groan and lugged it to the front of the train.

"Oh, Yuriko-chan, you have grown to be such a nice young

lady," My cousin Naomi sang while hugging me. I tried to thank her but my voice was muffled. She let go, and I took a breath and replied again with a more audible, "Domo arigato, Naomi-san."

"What about me, Naomi-san? Have I grown?" Genji asked as he jumped up and down. I sighed, shook my head, and walked toward Naomi's car.

For the entire ride to Kisa we passed farm after farm growing vegetables. Dotted in between were cows and goats surrounded by the safety of a barbed-wire fence. On my first trip out here I found all the gardens and grazing farm animals fascinating. Now, all that occurred to me was there were no tall buildings, no shops, no bustling people, and most important of all, no Papa or Machiko. This was going to be a very boring place to stay.

We arrived at the country house in about twenty minutes, but it seemed more like hours. I had forgotten how small and very simple the farmhouse was. We hadn't stayed here for a couple summers. When we had been here in the past, Papa had vacationed with us the entire time. This time I had to wait until the weekend to see him.

I crinkled my nose and frowned. The house had a musty smell, so all the windows and the huge sliding front doors were opened. All I could think about was how easy it would be for snakes to slither in. I shuddered thinking about the first time I encountered a snake here under the sink.

I looked around the front living room. The tokonoma had

a pretty scroll with peach blossoms that Papa had brought the last time we were here. The only familiar objects were our family pictures that Papa had left here that time as well.

I went to the area where I would be sleeping and pulled out the picture of Papa I had packed. It was not the same as having him with me, but it was better than nothing at all. I looked out the window and saw cows and rows of corn. The shadows had begun to get longer, and I caught a glimpse of pink on the horizon. While I watched the cows eat, I wondered if Papa was sitting down to dinner yet, and if he was missing me.

Sumiyo's voice interrupted my thoughts. "Dinnertime, Yuriko-chan."

I walked the few feet to the dining area. The whole time, I scanned the tatami floor, watching for the first sign of a snake.

The dining area was next to the kitchen and it was very old-fashioned. The kitchen's porcelain sink still had a lever that we pumped when we wanted water to drink, cook, or wash. At least there was a gas stove for cooking and for heating the water we needed to bathe, but it was still very rustic.

After dinner, Aunt Kimiko and I brought out the futons from the oshiire, the bedding closet. We laid them out and placed our comforters on top. As the eldest, Sumiyo took the only bedroom. The rest of us slept in the living area. That was another reason for me to hate being here. In my own house, I had my own room. But in the country I had to sleep futon-to-futon with both Aunt Kimiko *and* Genji-chan!

What made matters worse was that Aunt Kimiko loved to tell ghost stories. During our last visit, she had told a story about an ancient samurai ghost who still lived in the house and would come out at night wielding his sword to hunt any children who were asleep. I had insisted on sleeping in Papa's room that night. The next day I announced, "I am not sleeping in that house again!"

Papa had said, "Joya, I have a solution. I will be back soon." He left and returned with a Shinto priest from the farm village. The Shinto priest stood in front of the house chanting a blessing and waving the Ōnusa—a wooden wand decorated with white paper cut in a zigzag pattern—slowly from left to right. With each sway of the Ōnusa, the white streamers made a gentle rustling sound.

When he finished he said, "Any evil spirits are now banished from this site." I agreed to go back into the house but refused to sleep anywhere except for in Papa's room.

Tonight, after Aunt Kimiko's story about the samurai ghost whose sword turned into a snake, Genji puffed up his chest and claimed he was not scared. However, he kept waking me up during the night asking if I heard any noises. He didn't know it, but I was also awake. I stayed up to make sure that a ghost snake did not slide into my futon and bite me while I slept. I was not sure if the Shinto priest's blessing had included snakes or not, so I wasn't going to take any chances. I lay in my futon, wishing that Papa were there.

CHAPTER TWENTY-FOUR

"Encouraging Reminder From Former Prime Minister Tojo, 'As Long As There Remains a Spirit of Loyalty and Patriotism There is Nothing to Fear.'"

Showa 20 May 11, NHK Radio morning broadcast

"Good morning, Yuriko-chan," Sumiyo said as she came out of her bedroom.

"Good morning, Sumiyo. Friday is finally here and Papa will be arriving soon!" I exclaimed as I finished folding my futon.

"I'm looking forward to seeing him, too. Come into the kitchen, and I will make you breakfast before we go to the train station to meet him."

"Sumiyo, would you mind if I was the first one to welcome Papa? You could drop me off before he arrives. I'm sure he'll want to walk after the long train ride. That's what he's done in the past. His arthritis is always worse after he sits a long time," I said, hoping she'd allow me that small amount of time with Papa alone.

Sumiyo nodded. "Of course, I do not mind. I know you and your papa need time together. I will drop you off. Then I can have lunch ready when you both return."

"Thank you, Sumiyo," I said, giving her a smile. "By the way, it seems much too quiet in here. Where are Aunt Kimiko and Genji?"

"They went for a walk to the pasture to visit the cows. They should be back soon."

Just at that moment, Aunt Kimiko burst into the kitchen holding Genji on her hip. Stray hairs were loose from her bun, swaying wildly on the top of her head. She seemed distressed and was out of breath.

Genji wailed, "Put me down, Mama! Put me down! I can run by myself!"

Sumiyo looked at me, raised her eyebrows, and then turned to Aunt Kimiko. "Is everything all right?"

"Naomi-san came out to the pasture and told me that the allies are victorious in Europe!" she said between breaths.

"Oh!" Sumiyo and I said in unison.

"It happened on May eighth, but was not announced right away," Aunt Kimiko said as she wiped the sweat from her brow.

"Does this mean the war is over in Europe?" I asked.

"Yes, it does. But not in Japan," Aunt Kimiko replied. "The

news report stated that Germany and Italy surrendered. But Japan would not do that." Aunt Kimiko attempted to flatten her hair with her hands. "Sumiyo-san, could you please help me fix my hair again? It fell out when I was running. And Yuriko-chan, please give Genji some breakfast." She and Sumiyo exited the kitchen toward the bedroom and I could hear them talking in hushed tones.

"Hungry, hungry, hungry . . ." Genji chanted as he sat at the table.

"Yes, I know, Genji. You only need to tell me once. Please, go wash your hands." As I ladled miso soup into a bowl, I thought about Germany surrendering. *They were Japan's ally, so now are we all on our own?* Papa had said Japan was running out of supplies. *How are we to make enough weapons or planes without any other countries to help us?* I hoped that the Emperor's divinity and the patriotism of Japan's people were enough to save us.

"Yuriko, my soup." Genji said as he poked me in the side, causing me to jump and spill some soup on to the counter.

"What? Oh. I'm sorry. Here it is." I placed the bowl on the kitchen table and began wiping the counter.

"What are you going to do today, Yuriko?"

"I am going to pick up my papa at the train station all by myself," I said.

"Can I come, too?"

"Absolutely not! You're too young. And like I said, I'm going *by myself.*"

Genji frowned and looked disappointed. Since I had some time before I left for the train station and could use something to take my mind off Germany's surrender, I generously offered, "But I *will* read *Norakura* to you before I leave for the station."

●●●

Sumiyo dropped me off a half hour before Papa's train was scheduled to arrive. While pacing inside the station, I spotted a newspaper stand. A newspaper article discussed a city named Berlin falling. I stopped to read further. Apparently for the city to fall, actual troops from the Soviet Union had fought land battles while the United States dropped bombs on the city. I thought back to last June when the United States fought in France against the Germans. *Would the Americans land here, too? Who would fight them here? Would the Emperor bring all our troops from the Pacific back to Japan to fight since there are not many left in the country? Or am I really going to have to learn better aim with a bamboo spear? What about gyokusai?* I paced again with my fists tapping against my legs.

My worries halted when I finally heard the much-anticipated song of the train's whistle and the clacking of wheels on the track before I saw the train round the bend. The screeching of the brakes caused me to cover my ears. As the smoke from the engine began to clear, I saw Papa step down from the first-class car. I ran to him. He placed his suitcase on the platform and held out both arms to envelope me in a hug. I could smell his aftershave, and a feeling of calm rushed over me. My world was right again.

"Joya, I am so happy to see you. How have you kept busy this week? I hope you were helpful to Sumiyo-san," Papa said, his eyes twinkling in the brilliant sunlight.

"Oh, Papa, I am so happy you are here! And I've been very busy this week. I helped pump water for our baths every night, and I am responsible for closing the large wooden doors each evening. I make sure that no snakes slither in while we are sleeping."

Papa laughed as he took my hand.

"I missed you so much, Papa! How was your week?"

"I spent most of my time at the newspaper. Did you hear that Germany surrendered and that the allies are victorious in Europe?" he asked.

"Yes, Aunt Kimiko told us this morning. Does that really mean the war in Europe is over?"

"Yes, Joya, it does."

"I wish it could be over here, too." I looked up at Papa.

He nodded his head as he squeezed my hand. And then, in silence, we began our walk back to the house. I decided that for the rest of the weekend, my only focus would be on spending time with my papa.

CHAPTER TWENTY-FIVE

"The Americans Have Attacked Kure Naval Base and Fierce Fighting is in Progress."

Showa 20 August 1 edition

After Germany surrendered, Papa told us that the Americans would now be more focused on the war against Japan. He was busier than ever at the office as more men from his company were being drafted into the army. After his short visit, Papa was only able to return to see us once more in late June.

Time in the country seemed to pass much slower than in the city. We all spent part of the mornings at my aunt and uncle's house, but after lunch, Sumiyo and I came back to our cottage. Aunt Kimiko and Genji spent a lot of time at a farm down the road from us because the family who lived there had a boy Genji's age. I enjoyed having some free time without being bothered by my annoying cousin.

I spent a lot of time reading and rereading the books I had

brought with me. I also wrote a few lines of a letter I would have sent to Machiko had the postal service still worked as it did before the war. Unfortunately, letters did not always get delivered anymore. So I kept this to give to her whenever we returned home.

Dear Machiko,

How are you and your family? How is the work at the plane factory? I heard about the Japanese balloon bomb that exploded in Oregon in the United States. Did your factory make any of these? I have been very busy (ha, ha). I spend my days reading my books and reading Norakuro to Genji. *I have read it so much that I now know it by heart! I have been playing card games with Sumiyo, too. She is teaching me how to play hanafuda. I never had any interest in it before, but it is actually a fun card game. Very exciting, neh? I'll have to teach it to you once I'm home.*

I miss being able to talk with you whenever I want. This is the longest we have gone without seeing each other. I am hoping we come home soon. Do you know anything more about the attack on Kure? I worry about Hiroshima Port and if . . .

"Yuriko, dinner is ready," Sumiyo called from the next room.

I folded the letter and put it in one of my books. I joined Sumiyo, Aunt Kimiko, and Genji at the kitchen table.

I looked out the window at the rain. "I miss Papa." I sighed.

Sumiyo placed her chopsticks on her hashioki and said, "I do, too, Yuriko-chan. I believe it is time for us to return home to Hiroshima."

I turned from looking out the window and exclaimed, "We can go home to Papa? Really?"

"Hooray!" Even Genji had finally lost interest in day after day of cows in the pasture.

"I can't wait to see Machiko, too! I have to hear all about her work at the plane factory," I said. I got up and began to bring the empty dishes to the sink.

"Well, it definitely is too quiet around here," Aunt Kimiko agreed.

Sumiyo stood up from the table and said, "Good. Then the decision has been made, and we will leave tomorrow morning. We will arrive in time to surprise your papa when he gets home from the office."

The thought of going home to be with Papa and Machiko kept a smile on my face for the rest of the evening.

The next morning we were all up with the roosters, ready to head home.

"Yuriko-chan, is your suitcase packed?" Sumiyo asked.

"Yes, Sumiyo-san."

"Could you please help Genji-chan put his in the car? Your Aunt Kimiko and I will follow as soon as we do one last check to be sure nothing is left behind."

"Come with me, Genji," I said as I picked up my suitcase in my right hand and his in my left.

It rained the entire train ride to Hiroshima, but I wouldn't let that dampen my spirits.

●●●

"You are not supposed to be here. You should all still be at the country house." Papa's voice grew louder and his lips faded into a thin line as he stood in the entryway to our home, clearly perplexed as to why we were back. But the look in his eyes softened as he spoke. I ran, throwing my arms around him, and squeezing tightly. He looked down at me and said, "Well, prepare to go back to the farm this weekend." His voice sounded gruff, but that didn't stop him from hugging me tightly, too.

That night I went to bed early with a bad headache and stomach cramps. The next couple of days were a blur as I was either sleeping or throwing up into a bucket. Papa and Sumiyo took turns watching over me. The only good thing about being sick was not returning to the country house that weekend, as I was too weak to make the train ride there.

On Monday morning, Papa entered my room early. "Joya, Joya, wake up."

I rolled over to face him. He was standing in the doorway. "Yes, Papa?"

"How are you feeling today?"

I sat up and said, "Well, my head does not hurt finally. And I have not thrown up since yesterday afternoon."

"That is good. I am happy to hear this. You will be excused today from going into the center of town with the rest of your classmates. You can return tomorrow to assist them in demolishing the wooden buildings. You should go outside today to get some fresh air."

"Yes, Papa. It will be nice to get out of this room. But what time is it? Why are you leaving so early? You do not usually leave for the office until noon."

"I am going to purchase a train ticket for one of the reporters at the newspaper. He needs to visit his injured son."

"Oh. I hope his son will be okay. Papa, will you be home earlier today since you are going in earlier? Now that I am feeling better, I would love to play hanafuda with you."

"Hanafuda? I thought you did not care for card games?"

"Well, Sumiyo taught me while we were in the country, and I found I actually like it." I smiled and shrugged my shoulders.

"That sounds like a wonderful plan. I will make sure I return early in the afternoon."

I stood up and he walked over to me. He kissed my forehead. As he headed toward my door, I asked, "Papa, you are not still mad that I am home, are you?"

He turned back to me with a smile that crinkled the corner of his eyes and said, "Joya, I am always happiest when you are here with me. I was angry because I worried about the safety of my family. But I agree with Sumiyo. It was time you returned. I was very lonely."

"I am so glad, Papa!" I ran and hugged him, and he

squeezed me tightly back.

"Joya, I will see you in a few hours, neh?"

"Yes, see you then, Papa."

After he left, I got back under the covers and read for a short time. Around 7:30 a.m. I decided to get dressed—something I hadn't done in almost a week. I pulled on a shirt and monpe pants, and I attempted to smooth some of my unruly hair back into the braids I'd slept in. I glanced at my reflection in the mirror. I would not win a beauty prize, but at least I looked presentable.

Downstairs in the kitchen, I took one look at the breakfast on the table, and my stomach reeled as if filled with ocean waves. I decided to skip breakfast and have tea instead. As I finished my cup of tea, I spotted Machiko across the street hanging laundry. She was working the afternoon shift at the factory, and if I wanted to speak with her, I needed to do it that morning. I slipped on my shoes and ran out to catch her before she went inside.

"Machiko, ohayo!" I bent over with my hands on my knees to take deep breaths. When would I realize that my body was not meant to run—especially so soon after being sick? The hot August morning air clung to my skin, making breathing even more difficult.

Machiko turned around. "Good morning, Yuriko!" She gave me a hug. "I'm so happy to see you! It's been a long two months without you. But aren't you supposed to be going back to the country?"

I attempted to catch my breath. "Papa decided Sumiyo is as stubborn as he is and that we don't have to go back."

Just then, B-sans flew overhead. We both looked up at the sky. There was no siren blaring. A voice from the loudspeaker perched on a pole at the front of the house announced that it was only a weather plane. And weather planes were not a threat as they had never been used in an attack.

After the announcement I began to speak again. "Machiko, can we listen to some jazz this morning before you go to work?"

The deafening hum of a low-flying plane drowned out Machiko's reply. This time a siren sounded. The hair lifted on the back of my neck.

An ear-shattering popping noise.

An intense burst of white light.

The ground trembled and opened beneath us, as if to swallow us whole. Machiko and I clung to each other and screamed.

Darkness . . .

CHAPTER TWENTY-SIX

*"PLEASE BE SURE ALL FAMILY MEMBERS ORDER
THE CORRECT GAS MASK SIZE."*

Neighborhood Association poster

I opened my eyes and immediately began to cough. I wiped away dirt and rocks from inside my mouth and on my face. My head pounded as if someone had beaten it like a taiko drum. Reaching up, I touched my head and felt a lump. I looked down at my hand to see if I was bleeding, but it was too dark to see anything. *How much time had passed? Was I dead? What had happened? Was it an earthquake?* I tried to piece things together. *I heard a plane engine. But it was a weather plane. Wait! There was a second plane—there was a siren. That plane must have dropped a bomb! I was talking with someone, but was it Sumiyo? No, it was Machiko!*

"Machiko? Machiko, are you all right?" I called out into the darkness.

"Yuriko, Yur-i-ko." Her voice was so faint. It was as if she was whispering. "Help me, Yuriko." Some rocks shifted and I heard Machiko groan.

"Are you hurt?" I called, still unable to see where she was.

"I can't move, Yuriko." Machiko's teeth clicked together in between her words. "It's so very cold." She began to cry.

"I am coming. I *will* find you. Please, don't cry." I tried to push away the wood and dirt surrounding me. "Keep talking to me so I can follow your voice." I heard no reply. Droplets of sweat stung my eyes. My heart was racing and my hands clawed at the debris, hoping the next rock I removed would reveal my best friend.

"Machiko, I am going to find you and soon we will be in your room, listening to some jazz." I continued to talk, hoping to calm her. But it was more to calm myself. If I kept talking to her, that meant she was still alive and that I would find her.

My fingers throbbed. I tried to open my hands wider to rip away more rocks with each swipe. Every time I did, I scraped against jagged edges. Moisture oozed down my hand. I knew it must be blood even if I could not see it. I called out to her again. "Machiko, I need to rest for a few minutes. I will dig some more. I just need to rest my hands." I closed my eyes and my cheeks were wet. Not from blood, but from tears. My whole body shivered.

I must have passed out. When I awoke with a start—as soon as I attempted to move—searing pain coursed through my body. I did not know how long I had been unconscious, but I suddenly remembered what I had been doing.

"Machiko, I am so sorry. You know me—daydreaming again." I kept calling to her while I forced my body to move. I tried again to dig toward where I had last heard her voice.

"Machiko, please talk to me. I know I can find you." The back of my throat burned. I swallowed the urge to cry again. Crying would not help me dig any faster.

Silence.

I could not see anything. Maybe I was dead after all.

Then I heard a voice. "Yuriko, Yuriko, are you there?"

It was not Machiko's, but a voice from outside of the debris. Some wood shifted in front of me. Again I heard, "Yuriko, Yuriko, please answer me!"

I recognized that voice. It was Sumiyo! She was alive! I began to move toward the hole. "Sumiyo! I hear you! I'm under here. Can you hear me?"

"Yuriko! Come out!" More dust enveloped me. Something fell to the ground. I stopped.

"I cannot move any further! If I do the rest of this will fall on me. And there's Machiko—I cannot leave her!"

"No, Yuriko, I am right here to pull you out. Trust me!"

"Sumiyo, I cannot leave Machiko. I know I am close to her. Help me dig her out, please!" I heard the desperation in my voice.

"Yuriko, trust me. Once you are safe, then we can dig her out," Sumiyo pleaded.

I began to push away more rocks around the hole. I could

hear Sumiyo pulling off heavier pieces of wood and stone on her side, but it did not seem to make any difference. I screamed and pounded at the rubble in front of me. Saving Machiko depended on me getting out first. I could hear Sumiyo, which meant I had to be close to the surface. Why was this so hard?

It felt like hours went by. And still, the rocks and wood were endless.

Finally, Sumiyo's hand appeared through the hole. As I grasped it, I noticed that her hands, which had once been so graceful and soft, were bloodied and raw.

I crawled through the hole, coughing hard. Dust settled around me and I looked up. The sky was no longer blue, but shades of purple, orange, and brown. In another time and in another place, I might have thought the color combination beautiful. But now it seemed ominous and deadly.

A thin veil of smoke hung over the landscape. Sumiyo put her hand on my shoulder and turned me to face her. That was when I noticed she was bleeding from her cheek and the side of her head. Her once elegantly coiffed hair resembled a bird's nest. Her monpe pants were torn at her thigh. Yet she still managed to look happy, and I knew it was because I was safe.

I looked in the direction of my house. The outside frame was the only thing left standing. Every room seemed to have crumbled to the floor below. I recognized the two cement pillars where the iron gates had been, but the cement walls were reduced to ashes. My home was gone, as were all the other houses on my street, as far as I could see.

I would have time to grieve later. Now I needed to rescue my best friend.

"Machiko, I am out. Call to me. Tell me where you are!" I screamed. My entire body shook as if it were twenty degrees outside and I was without a winter coat. It was then that I realized I was not the only one screaming. I heard people shouting at piles of rubble all the way down our street. They shouted out names of family members presumably trapped under the remnants of what were once their homes. Many were met with silence. And so was I.

I refused to accept it. I heaved pieces of roof tiles and handfuls of dirt at a frantic pace. I heard the drone of a plane flying in our direction. Sumiyo gripped my arm and her voice shrieked, "We need to go *now*! There is nothing more we can do. There could be more bombs coming. We must get away."

As soon as she finished saying this, another plane dropped a black sticky substance that looked like raindrops made of tar.

"I cannot leave her. I need to save Machiko!" I knew my tone of voice was disrespectful but all I could think about was saving my friend.

Someone yelled, "They are pouring oil on us to burn us even more!"

After hearing that, Sumiyo picked me up and began carrying me away. At first I was so surprised she did this, I could not speak, could not move. Then I started screaming Machiko's name. My eyes were riveted on the wreckage behind us. Sumiyo took me toward our home, where just a few hours earlier I had heard our koi pond burbling and the bamboo peacefully click-clacking.

The drops of oil stopped as suddenly as they had begun. The planes disappeared. I was still watching the mountain of dirt and concrete that held my best friend beneath it, when out of the corner of my eye I noticed a sinister orange and red glow above the center of town. Fire whirled around like a typhoon, lighting up the darkness. I could not look away. All I could think about was that my papa was in the middle of that fire.

That was my last thought before the world went black.

CHAPTER TWENTY-SEVEN

*"PREPARE FOR FINAL BATTLE
ON IMPERIAL SOIL."*

Propaganda poster

I winced at the pain that shot through my head as I opened my eyes. I looked up and noticed a torn, dirty sheet tented above me. Why is that there? I sat up and touched the top of my head where it hurt the most. I felt some fabric wrapped around it. The dusty haze and devastation jolted my memory.

"Papa! Machiko!" I screamed. My stomach heaved, and I threw up.

Sumiyo ran toward me, stopped, looked behind her, and yelled, "It is Yuriko-chan! She is awake now. She is okay."

Yet I felt anything but okay.

Sumiyo sat next to me, tore what looked to be a remnant of a kimono, and began to wipe my face. "Ah, Yuriko-chan, you are awake."

"Did I faint?"

"Yes, but just for a short while. Maybe two hours. It is hard to really know the exact time without clocks and with an evening sky during the day. Let me clean your cuts and wrap your arms. They are still bleeding and must hurt an awful lot."

"No, Sumiyo, I am fine. Please take care of yourself first. You are bleeding, too."

Out of the dust and smoke, Aunt Kimiko came walking toward us. She had Genji in her arms. Her hair was matted and her face was bloody. Her red hands hugged Genji close to her. He wasn't moving.

"Kimiko-san! You are alive! How is Genji-chan?" Sumiyo asked as she ran over to Aunt Kimiko.

"Thankfully, he is alive, but he is so quiet. His eyes are tearing; he seems to be in shock. Where is Yuriko-chan?"

"I am right here!" I shouted, feeling a sense of relief that both Aunt Kimiko and Genji were here. "Was Papa with you? Where is Fumi-san?" It sounded more like pleading than a question.

Sumiyo shook her head from side to side. "Fumi-san, she . . . she did not make it out of the house in time. I have not seen your papa."

"How can this be happening?" I cried out.

Sumiyo touched my shoulder, but I turned away and began to limp toward the ruins where I had last heard Machiko's voice.

Darkness covered us like a blanket attempting to hide the

horror we were facing. Eerie blue lights shined on the rubble that was once sidewalks or streets. The macabre orbs were not from any gas lamp. They were from the many funeral pyres that dotted the land where houses from our neighborhood once stood. I saw an outline of someone where Machiko's house used to be. I moved closer and recognized her father. I stopped behind him, not wanting to intrude. I heard him speaking to the dirt while clutching a piece of fabric. I craned my neck and recognized the fabric he held. It was Machiko's blouse that she wore this morning. My hands balled into fists at my side as a chill traveled down the middle of my back. My mouth went dry and my cry was barely audible. "No, no, no, Machiko. I am so sorry. How will I live without you?"

Machiko's father lit a match and threw it on top of some piled wood, saying "Oyasumi nasai, Machiko-chan. Take care of your mama and brothers. We will meet again." He began singing a lullaby. I couldn't take it anymore. I sobbed as I staggered back to our camp.

"Yuriko-chan, what happened?" Sumiyo met me and put her arm around my shoulder.

I couldn't speak. I just looked in the direction of Machiko's father and the blue fire. Sumiyo followed my gaze and a tear fell down her cheek. She led me to an area where one of the neighbors had erected a makeshift tent. Under it, Aunt Kimiko lay on her side hugging Genji close to her. Aunt Kimiko opened her eyes and sat up as we approached. Sumiyo and I sat next to her. Sumiyo shook her head at Aunt Kimiko.

They both put a hand on each of my shoulders. No one spoke a word. Our entire tent area was quiet. Our glazed, bloodshot eyes stared at each other as if in a trance. What was the point of speaking?

I pulled my knees up, rested my chin on them, and closed my eyes. I willed myself to picture Machiko and me dancing at Sakura Hanami only a few months ago—instead of the image of her father lighting that match.

At some point that night, I fell asleep, exhausted. I woke up to Sumiyo shaking me by the shoulder. "Come, it's light out—we need to go find your papa."

My eyes popped open at the sound of his name. "I am ready."

Aunt Kimiko walked under the tent with Genji in her arms.

"Aunt Kimiko, are you coming with us?" I asked as I moved toward her and rubbed Genji's back.

"No, I will stay here. Genji is sleeping at last. It will be good to have someone here in case your papa comes back to the house." Sumiyo and I turned on instinct toward our home. Our eyes met at the same time when we realized that there was no home left. Not even one room was intact. Pieces of shattered glass and shredded, charred bits of tatami spread out in front of us. Oddly enough, some bamboo remained where our backyard used to be. Strange white lines dotted their front side. The bamboo slanted backwards as if bent from a strong wind. Tattered fabric tents set up on either side of what was once our road. Iron from what may have been a stove lay crumpled like paper in a trash can. Nothing was recognizable. It reminded me of pictures of Tokyo from after the firebomb this past March.

Sumiyo took my hand and we headed toward the direction we thought would lead to the center of town. It was confusing since we no longer had any landmarks for judging distance. The roads were hills of rocks and cement. This made it difficult to walk as well. I did not care about the pounding in my head or the pain in my arms or my legs as I walked. I was determined to bring Papa back to safety. I would have plenty of time to feel pain later.

Fog from the smoldering embers and funeral pyres surrounded us. Incessant buzzing from the flies droned in our ears. The insects swirled around like dust shaken from tatami mats when they were being cleaned. With each breath, I inhaled the acrid stench of charred wood and bodies. I wondered if I would I ever smell the cherry blossoms' fragrance again. As I looked around, the one word that came to mind was *Jigoku*—Hell. If *Jigoku* existed, this was what it must look and smell like.

People walked past us and their faces looked dead. They looked neither scared nor sad. No one acknowledged each other. They walked as if their main purpose was to keep moving—like mummies in a Hollywood movie. Some collapsed, but the rest of the death walkers continued to march forward. They stepped over the fallen bodies without ever looking down. I tried my best to not fall over the rubble or broken bodies as I kept up with Sumiyo's pace.

"Ishikawa-san, Ishikawa-san," a familiar voice called to us. We turned to see Okada-san, an employee at Papa's newspaper, stumbling toward us. He was out of breath. Gashes on his forehead and face were bleeding. His shirtsleeve hung off his shoulder, exposing a blistering burn on his arm. Yet he sounded joyful as he called our name. "I have seen Ishikawa-san. He is at the train station."

"Is he hurt?"

"Is he alive?"

Both Sumiyo and I spoke in unison. As I waited for answers, I held my breath. My stomach swarmed with butterflies.

"Hai, he is alive. He is injured, but I spoke to him. He wanted me to find his family, to make sure you are all right. He was very thirsty, but I told him not to move. There is no water safe to drink, but at least now I have found both of you." As Okada-san spoke, he caressed the bloodstained hair on top of my head as tears streamed down his cheeks.

"We must go to him!" I cried.

"Of course, of course, follow me."

It seemed as if we walked for hours. I no longer noticed anything around me—the funeral pyres, the dead bodies, those walking about like ghosts. I stared straight ahead with my one goal of finding my papa.

I came to an abrupt stop when I felt a tug at my sleeve and heard a small voice call out, "Please, help me. Help me find my mother."

I turned to look behind me, expecting to see a toddler. Instead, I was looking at some demon. Its face was like molten lava. I could not tell if it was a boy or a girl. There was nothing left on this poor creature to identify it as a human being. I pulled my shirt out of what was left of its hand and screamed as I ran away.

I ran straight into Sumiyo. She saw what I ran from and embraced me. I looked up at her face. She opened her mouth as if to say something, but quickly closed it. Tears made cracks on her dirt-covered cheeks. She had no words that would comfort me or explain what we had just seen. We could only push forward. Papa waited for us.

As I looked at the ruins around me, I could not imagine how we would find the train station. All the buildings were either leveled or mere shells. My palms began to sweat, and my head swooned like the time I was so frightened by the rat snake. What if Papa was under the fallen buildings? I pushed that out of my thoughts as Okada-san came to a stop.

The ruins of the train station stood before us—twisted metal smoldered in a heap. I looked around.

"Where is Papa? He was supposed to be here!" I wailed as I looked around at some of the dead bodies and blurry, whitish gray shadows on the platform.

Okada-san replied with urgency in his voice, "Ishikawa-san was right here. I used this rock as a pillow for him to rest on when I left him to find you." He continued to point at the rock and did not look at us. "I told him not to move. He was right here. He was right here."

"He must have been well enough to move and decided to find us himself," I said. Okada-san did not answer. He shook his head from side to side and continued to stare at the rock pillow he had evidently made for Papa.

Sumiyo spoke in her calm, soothing tone, "Thank you very much for all your assistance, Okada-san. Please go, and find your own family. I hope they are all well." She touched his arm and continued, "There is a shrine not far from here. Well, there *was* a shrine not far from here. Yuriko-chan and I will go there and pray to find her papa."

Okada-san bowed low. As I bowed in return, I thought about his family and how worried they must be for him while he was out helping us. As Sumiyo and I turned in the direction of the shrine, I hoped he still *had* a family waiting for him.

CHAPTER TWENTY-EIGHT

"To Deal the Foe the Final Blow."

Propaganda poster

I held tightly to Sumiyo's hand as we left the shell of what was once a bustling train station. I kept hoping to see Papa walking toward us with every step we took. I squeezed Sumiyo's hand as a silent sign of hope. She squeezed my hand in return.

Sumiyo tripped over some concrete steps. I grabbed her arm to steady her. She gasped, "Your papa—he is right here."

My heart pounded hard in my chest. I looked up; in my excitement I had not noticed that Sumiyo was looking at the ground and not ahead of her. She had not tripped on a step, but rather on Papa!

I looked down and saw a person whose head was twice its normal size and was flushed in a strange shade of blue. At first glance I thought Sumiyo was mistaken. But then I looked closer and recognized the three-piece suit he had worn that morning when he left home. I could see some of the familiarity of his facial features as I stared at his head more closely.

I forced myself to utter, "Is he alive?"

Sumiyo checked his neck for a pulse. "Yes! There is a faint pulse!" She smiled, and for the first time that day her voice held some hope. "We need to bring him back to our house. There will be help for him there. But your papa is a big man, and you and I alone cannot carry him."

Then the familiar voice of Okada-san sounded behind us: "I could not give up on Ishikawa-san so I followed you here. I think I saw a wheelbarrow on my way here. Let me see if I can get it so we can get him home."

In a matter of minutes Okada-san had returned with a small wheelbarrow. He and Sumiyo struggled, but managed to lift Papa's six-foot frame into the cart.

That was when I noticed that Papa's tie was loosened and his shoes were gone. His feet were engorged. In the vest where he once carried a pocket watch was a strange wound that looked like a hole, which seemed to be melting his skin. Sumiyo placed Papa's hand in the wagon and covered the wound I had been staring at with part of his vest. Okada-san pushed the cart over crumbled concrete and melted tar to where our neighborhood once stood. We passed what was left of our city hospital. So many burned victims waited in line along the one wall of the building that remained.

My fists tapped at my legs as I repeated in my head, "Papa will be fine, Papa will be fine." I heard a moan. Papa's head fell to the side, and his arm dangled off the wagon.

"*No!*" Sumiyo-san began to sob. It seemed as if I were watching a movie play out in front of me. Okada-san reached down and pressed his finger against Papa's neck. Then he touched Papa's wrist and shook his head at Sumiyo-san. He turned around, and I saw him wipe his eyes with his hands.

I looked at Papa's lifeless body in the wheelbarrow, with his head the color of navy blue and enlarged like a blowfish. But I didn't see that man. Instead, I saw my papa dressed in his handsome three-piece suit, Panama hat, and shoes that he personally shined with great care. Later, I did not see him on the funeral pyre where Sumiyo sat with him. I saw him walking away, proudly twirling his walking stick as he did when he walked me to school.

Loneliness spread through me like a poison. I tried to imagine Papa hugging me in a loving embrace. I strained to smell the scent of his cologne. I wanted to sob until I could no longer breathe. But the tears would not fall. It was as if the intense heat of the blast had dried them all up.

CHAPTER TWENTY-NINE

*"THE ENEMY HAS USED A NEW BOMB IN IHE
ATTACK OF HIROSHIMA. DETAILS ARE STILL
UNDER INVESTIGATION."*

Showa 20 August 10 edition

Aunt Kimiko and Sumiyo set up cots for our family along with two other families in the basement of an undamaged school a few miles away. Even though there were fifteen of us in the small space, it wasn't noisy. I had lost Papa and Machiko. The others had lost family members as well. Our homes and the lives that we once led were decimated. There was nothing to talk about. Even Genji was silent—he had not spoken since the bomb dropped. I felt so guilty for all the times I wished he would stop talking to me.

We did not have running water for the first day after the bomb fell. We could not even use the river for washing. The water rippled with burnt corpses. Relief workers brought notices that the water company's treatment plant, which was located about two miles away, was thankfully operational. Some boys from the neighborhood left to bring back containers of water for us to drink and cook with.

Food was scarce. Aunt Kimiko and one of our neighbor's older sons walked to a farmhouse a few miles up the road to bring back some rice and vegetables. Each person was allotted a small amount of food. We didn't know how long we had to make the food last. Aunt Kimiko gave half of her allotment to Genji, and sometimes I did as well.

I do not know where someone got a radio, but one appeared a few days after the bombing. That was how we found out that the United States had used a special type of bomb on us for the first time. They called it "the atomic bomb" and it was the weapon that had killed the people I loved and had taken away my home. We referred to it as *pika don*, bright light and thunderous noise. We learned that the same type of bomb was also dropped on the city of Nagasaki three days after Hiroshima was destroyed.

One week later, I, along with everyone left on our street, gathered around the radio to listen to our Emperor's voice: "We have endured hardships and sadness, but we have been defeated by that atomic bomb, and all Japanese could be injured or killed. It is too pitiful for even one of my dear subjects to be killed. I do not care what happens to me."

The war was over, and we had lost. The Japanese people finally heard what our Emperor's voice sounded like and it was to announce Japan's defeat in the Greater East Asian War. After his speech, people in the room began to chatter and to express their relief at finally having peace. They could begin rebuilding their homes and, perhaps, their lives.

I did not care about rebuilding my life without Papa or Machiko. How could I rebuild something I could never get back?

A few days after the broadcast of Japan's surrender, a telegram arrived for Aunt Kimiko. We held our breath, knowing it was about Akira-san. *Please let him only be injured*, I thought, squeezing my eyes shut as she read the telegram. She began to cry as she crumpled the paper and let it fall to the floor. She turned to go lay near Genji, who was napping. I scooped up the paper and smoothed it out as best as I could. Akira-san was dead. He died in the Philippines at the beginning of August before the *pika don* was dropped.

I could feel nothing. I did love Akira-san—not as my papa, but as an uncle or older brother. But I still couldn't cry. I looked over at Aunt Kimiko, who wept while rubbing Genji's back. Even though I had never gotten along with Aunt Kimiko, my heart ached for her and her loss, too.

●●●

Our neighbors, who had lived at the far end of our street, left the school's basement within a couple weeks. They were carpenters and had built a temporary home on their former property. When their home was done, they began to work on building an interim shelter for us where our house had once stood. Once they cleared the land of debris, they stumbled upon the one salvageable item: Papa's safe. It was melted but still intact. It had been forced open and emptied. People were desperate and robberies were common. We weren't surprised, but still, I felt even more defeated.

Fragments of metal, cement pieces, and wood debris were removed from our yard. The neighbors dug a foundation for us. Aunt Kimiko, Sumiyo, and I took turns helping them dig. But today there were enough men, and they let me rest. I sat and watched them the entire time—not because I was that interested, but because it stopped me from thinking about the fact that Papa and Machiko were gone and I was still alive. It was easier than having a conversation with anyone.

It was while I was watching that I heard the clink of metal hitting metal and went to see what the shovels had found. A man continued to dig the dirt that surrounded what looked like a black piece of metal. Once he dug away enough dirt, he bent over and pushed away the remaining dirt with his hands.

"It looks like part of an iron gate," he said.

I moved forward and started to move the dirt myself. "It is our front gate!" I exclaimed. "How did it get here? I thought the NA took it down to melt so it could be used to build planes. Why is it where the shrubs were planted?" Thoughts flooded back to me of that night I went out on the veranda and saw workmen digging. Papa said it was for new shrubs, but he had actually had other plans. I smiled. Even if he was not here physically, a piece of his stubborn personality endured in the form of our front gate.

One of the workers spoke. "Well, Yuriko-chan, that is definitely not the roots of a shrub!" The man chuckled and looked at me. That face looked so familiar. It dawned on me—it was the same Korean man who had been in my kitchen not so long ago.

"It's you—hello again!" I said, cracking my first smile since the bomb dropped.

"Hello, Yuriko-chan. I had much respect for your papa. He gave me a place to sleep that night and a job in the mail room at the newspaper, and now I have my own painting company. It is an honor to help rebuild your home. It appears that Ishikawa-san did not like the idea of donating all the iron, metal, and gold he owned."

I nodded with enthusiasm and picked up a shovel. "Please keep digging so we can see what else might be buried!"

After a few minutes of digging and scraping, I spotted a box wrapped with a red calico print furoshiki. I knelt down and pulled it from the dirt. Unwrapping the cloth and opening the wooden box, I saw that it held a silver frame with a picture of Papa and me on Children's Day when I was four, Papa's wedding ring, and gold earrings that had belonged to my mama—well, the woman that *I* knew as my mother. Nothing else. It wasn't much, but it was all the possessions my family had left. I clutched them to my chest and a deep sob escaped my lips.

CHAPTER THIRTY

"Japan's Foreign Affair Minister Signs the Japanese Instrument of Surrender Aboard the USS Missouri."

Showa 20 September 2 edition

"Noooooo!" I sat up straight on my cot. My pajamas stuck to my skin. I gulped air into my lungs as the room spun.

"Yuriko-chan, are you all right?" Within seconds, Sumiyo was next to me on the bed, holding me tight. "Was it the dream you keep having about your papa or Machiko?"

I wiped away tears with my damp sleeve. "It was about the child who looked as if he was melting. He asked me to find his mother. I should have helped him. Instead, I ran and left him all alone. All I see in the dream is his charred face asking me for help." I turned my head into Sumiyo's shoulder. She rocked me back and forth while patting my back.

"Yuriko-chan, you are not to blame. There was nothing

you or anyone could have done. As soon as you ran into my arms, that little boy fell to the ground. He died, Yuriko. He was going to die whether you helped him or not. You had every right to be frightened. We all saw things that day we had never imagined possible and hope to never see again." Her voice became a whisper with her last few words.

We sat on my cot in silence and I felt her tears on my face. I must have fallen asleep at some point because I woke up alone on my cot. I looked to my left and found Sumiyo asleep in a chair beside me. She had become part of my family less than a year ago, but she cared about me so much. To think I worried about having her as part of the family, and now she was my closest family member.

"Sumiyo, ohayo," I said and patted her hand.

Sumiyo sat up straighter and said, "Ah, ohayo. I am glad you were able to sleep after your nightmare."

"Thank you for staying with me. I am sorry you had to sleep in such an uncomfortable chair."

"I did not want to leave you in case you had another bad dream. I was not too uncomfortable. Actually, it was no worse than the cots. I will check what we have for breakfast and let you know when it is ready." She walked over to me, gave me a hug, and went into the kitchen area.

I reached for the box under my bed. I opened the cover to look at the items we had found buried in our yard. I ran my finger over the silver picture frame, and clutched a pair of gold earrings and Papa's wedding band to my heart. I imagined Papa as he packed these items, refusing to give them away to help the army battle the Americans. Battles we lost in the end anyway. *Did he sense that was going to happen?*

I looked at Papa and myself in the days before I knew what the word "war" meant. I studied the picture every day. I feared I would forget his smile or the sound of his voice and its booming timbre as he called my name when he came home at the end of the day. As I bent down to lose myself in the picture, I noticed a clump of hair on my pillow. I got up and grabbed the small mirror Sumiyo had found in our yard. To my horror, my eyebrows were gone! My face looked swollen, as if I had the mumps. And my eyes had permanent black smudges under each one from lack of sleep.

"AAH!" I cried.

"Yuriko-chan?" Sumiyo said, shuffling into the room.

"Oh! Sumiyo, look at me! I look horrible!"

"Yuriko-chan, it's going to be all right." She sat and put her arms around me. "A swollen face and hair loss seems to be very common right now. Remember, Aunt Kimiko and Genji had the same symptoms, but the doctor helped them. He will help you, too. I will call him after breakfast. This way he can see you before we go up to the country house. Your aunt and uncle want us to stay with them while our temporary home is being built."

"Thank you, Sumiyo. Are you sure I will be okay?"

"Hai, I will make the call to the doctor now. Why don't you begin to pack your things?"

Well, I knew that wouldn't take long. I no longer have much to pack. I can't remember when I was so excited to stay at the country house. A change of scenery would be so welcomed. No matter what the weather was or how much rebuilding had begun, all I saw here was death.

I dressed in my one pair of monpe pants and a blouse one of our neighbors gave me. I went out of the room and ate some rice. My jaw hurt as I chewed, but I was so hungry I finished the rice despite the pain. Someone knocked just as I placed my chopsticks on the hashioki, and it was Dr. Sata.

Sumiyo sat next to me and whispered, "Do not worry. The doctor will be able to help you."

Dr. Sata said, "Yuriko-chan, I have some capsules for you to take twice a day. You might not get your eyebrows back, but the swelling in your face should diminish." He said nothing about the hair on my head growing back, though.

I heard him say quietly to Sumiyo, "As long as she does not develop blue spots on her body, she should fully recover." I made a note to start a daily check for blue spots. After he left, Sumiyo and I gathered our one bag to begin our walk to the local streetcar that was still running. As we left our hovel, Aunt Kimiko and Genji arrived. Aunt Kimiko held Genji, who still hadn't spoken since the bomb dropped. I noticed Aunt Kimiko had no bag with her.

"You are not bringing anything?" I asked.

"We are not going with you to Aunt and Uncle's cottage," she said in an emotionless voice.

"But, why not?"

"We will be picked up tomorrow. Akira-san's family will be coming to get us and we will be going to live with them. I want to get as far away from Hiroshima as possible. Maybe then Genji will speak again." She looked around in disgust at our burnt-out neighborhood that held only shells of beautiful homes that once lined the streets.

My throat went dry. I wasn't fond of Aunt Kimiko and Genji, that's true. There were times over the past few years that I actually hated them. But as much as I may have wished it, being separated from them was something I never considered.

"Oh, of course you would go to Akira-san's family." My eyes watered thinking of Akira-san's laugh. I didn't know what else to say. So, I walked over and hugged both Aunt Kimiko and Genji. I kissed the back of my cousin's head and whispered to him, "Take care, Genji." He opened his eyes, stared at me briefly, and then closed them again.

Sumiyo hugged Aunt Kimiko, too. As we were walking away, Aunt Kimiko called to me, "Take care, Yuriko-chan." I turned to respond, but she had already disappeared inside the hovel.

Once we boarded the train, I leaned my head against the

back of the seat and closed my eyes. Sumiyo squeezed my hand and whispered, "It is all for the best. It will get better. We will live here again one day."

I nodded. I didn't want to tell her that I held no hope of a better life without Machiko or Papa.

CHAPTER THIRTY-ONE

*"TYPHOON MAKURAZAKI HEAVILY DAMAGES
HIROSHIMA CITY AREA LAST NIGHT."*

Showa 20 September 18, NHK Radio

Over the next two weeks, after we arrived at the cottage, I vomited daily. By the third week, I was able to drink liquids and eat rice without getting sick. We received a letter from Aunt Kimiko that she and Genji had moved to Akira-san's family home before the typhoon hit Hiroshima. Thankfully, they were safe. We also learned that our temporary house frame had been washed away in the waters that had flooded our neighborhood. We were not going back to the city anytime soon. I spent most of my days too exhausted to even care.

It took another week until the swelling in my face went away, leaving behind hollowed cheeks. Fuzzy hairs began to fill in the bald patches on my head. Each day I checked for any sign of my eyebrows growing back or if I had any blue spots. I overheard my aunt and Sumiyo's conversation one night when they thought I was asleep. Sumiyo told my aunt that once blue spots appear, death follows quickly. I didn't sleep at all that night.

One morning, Sumiyo interrupted my daily eyebrow and blue spot check. "I have good news, Yuriko-chan. You were accepted into the local high school, and they have room in the dormitory for you as well."

I did not reply or look up from the mirror. Sumiyo sat next to me and put her arm around my shoulders. Her fingers brushed my cheek and lifted my chin so I had to look into her eyes. She whispered, "Yuriko-chan, I know this is a very sad time. I loved him as well. However, I would dishonor him if I did not provide for you and send you back to school. Your education was very important to him. I cannot disappoint his spirit in that way."

I knew she was right, and I reluctantly nodded in agreement. I was lucky to test into that high school. It was two hours away from my home and was not damaged from the bomb. There was no other place I could go where I could get good housing and a good education. Uncle Daichi invited Sumiyo to stay at the cottage permanently and Aunt Kimiko made it clear she wasn't moving back. So I had no excuse not to go.

• • •

School would begin Monday, October 1. The weekend before, Sumiyo and I were the first ones to arrive at the dorm. Bunk beds lined two bare walls of the midsize room. A small rug sat in the middle of the tatami floor. A desk and lamp were standing in front of the window on the opposite wall. I looked over the room and said, "Well, it is no school basement, but it will do." We both laughed as we left our shoes at the doorway and entered.

"Let me help you unpack, and then I will leave you to meet your roommates. They should be arriving soon," Sumiyo said as she lifted my suitcase onto one bed. She unpacked the clothes that she helped me to sew. I made my bed with the quilts we brought from the cottage. I was glad Sumiyo convinced me to bring them because the only linen on each bed was a blue blanket. I placed the picture of Papa and me on one corner of the desk, and then we were done.

"The cab will be waiting for me. Will you walk me back to the front entrance, Yuriko-chan?"

"Of course."

As we left, two other girls and their families greeted us before they turned into the room. We greeted each other and smiled.

Sumiyo and I reached the main entrance. She turned to me. "Your papa would be so proud of you, Yuriko-chan. I am proud of you, too." Tears leaked out the corner of her eyes.

"Thank you for saying that, Sumiyo. I am grateful for all you have done for me. I love you." I hugged her and wiped tears from my eyes.

Sumiyo patted my back. "I love you too." She cleared her throat and said, "You will do fine. Your roommates will be very nice, I am sure. It is good that you will not be alone. I will write often, so remember to write me back."

"I will."

Sumiyo backed away, still holding on to my hand. She squeezed it before she finally let go and walked toward the cab. Before she got in, she stopped, turned back, and said, "Take care, Yuriko-chan."

I waved. She waved back, and when she did, the hem of her sleeve shifted, and I noticed two blue spots on her wrist. I stood there watching her cab drive away with a pit in my stomach. I knew in my heart I would not see Sumiyo again.

CHAPTER THIRTY-TWO

"First Time Women Allowed to Vote in the Upcoming April 10 General Election."

Showa 21 March 31 edition

My two roommates and I got along very well. Most of us at the school had experienced loss from the war in some way. One of my roommates had lost her mother to *pika don*, and the other had lost her brother at Pearl Harbor.

"Yuriko-chan, won't you come with us to the movies today?" one of my roommates asked. "Getting out of the dorm helps cheer us up. It would be good for you, too."

"I appreciate the invitation, but I am not ready to have fun yet." I forced a smile.

"Okay. We will be going again next weekend, and maybe then you will be ready." She patted my hand and the group of girls left me alone—the way I preferred it to be.

While they were gone, I played one of my roommate's

jazz records over and over again. With each note, I pictured Machiko that day when she had told me she had kept her jazz record. When I swayed to the beat, I closed my eyes and imagined her swaying next to me. It did not seem fair that I could spend time with other girls, but not with Machiko. Machiko and I could talk about anything. I had trusted her, and she had trusted me. *Will I ever be able to enjoy myself at school without her? What about all my classmates who died the day of the* pika don? *If Papa had sent me to school, I would be dead, too. Why am I alive and they are not? They would not get to experience high school or go to the movies ever again.*

Unfortunately, one of the people that I would have asked those questions lay buried beneath her home with her favorite jazz record.

So, I preferred to be by myself. It was safer that way. I hurt so much from losing Papa and Machiko that I decided it was better not to get close to anyone ever again. I would be alive, but I would not let myself feel any emotions. I became comfortable in my loneliness. I walked to stores in the center of town alone. I went to movies by myself. It did not even bother me when I got caught coming in after the eight o'clock curfew and the dorm mother reprimanded me, which was becoming more frequent.

One afternoon, the dorm mother called me to her office. "Yuriko-san, I have received a letter from the person who has been paying your tuition."

I knew it couldn't be Sumiyo. Within a month of being

dropped off at school, I received a letter from my aunt and uncle with the news of Sumiyo's death. My fear when I saw the spots proved true. One more loved one taken from me by the *pika don*.

"Is it a letter from my Uncle Daichi?" I asked.

"No, it is from a Nishimoto-san," she said plainly.

My mouth went dry and dropped open, but I managed to stammer, "My-my birth father?"

CHAPTER THIRTY-THREE

*"HOTOYAMA-SAN, LIBERAL PARTY WINS AND
THIRTY-NINE WOMEN ELECTED TO OFFICE
IN ELECTION!"*

Showa 21 April 10 edition

The emperor lost his divinity, a new school year began, women could now vote, and I was on a train to Hiroshima to meet my birth father. It amazed me that the sun still rose in the east.

The conductor took my ticket and I reclined in my seat. I thought about the events of the last few weeks. Nishimoto-san wrote to my school requesting that I move with him to Tokyo and continue my schooling there. A man I had only learned was my real father a year ago chose now to meet me. *Where was he before? Just because he has been paying my tuition since Sumiyo passed away didn't mean he could just have me move all the way to Tokyo with him and his new wife, did it?*

I winced. My head ached, and I felt dizzy. I had agreed to

meet him because I had so many unanswered questions. After all, what could it hurt? I couldn't feel any more depressed or disillusioned than I already did every day.

Then again, I didn't have to go to Tokyo. I had another option. I hadn't slept much the night before, tossing the idea around in my head, wondering if I had the courage. My exhaustion caught up with me and the rhythm of the train lulled me to sleep.

I woke to the conductor tapping me on the shoulder. "This is your stop, Miss."

I sat up. "Arigato gozaimasu!" I took my bag from the seat next to me and stepped off the train. I looked around the platform where I had once hoped to find Papa. My eyes prickled with tears. I took a deep breath in and let it out slowly. *Will these memories ever fade?* People walked to work, streetcars were in service, but I only saw fire, darkness, death. I glanced at my watch. I wasn't meeting Nishimoto-san until later in the afternoon. There was plenty of time. I had people to visit and decisions to make.

I took a streetcar toward the neighborhood where my home used to be. I passed the nearly bare cherry blossom trees. Newspapers had said nothing would grow for many years after the *pika don* and yet, here they were, blossoming ever so slightly. I inhaled but couldn't smell their fragrance, only smoke. There were some corrugated shacks set up in the old neighborhood, but nothing stood where my house used to be. I walked toward Machiko's plot of land, thumping my fists against my legs. I could feel the sweat dripping down my neck on the cool early spring morning. I stopped in front of the mound of dirt, wood, and memories. I placed my bag on the ground, unzipped it, and pulled out a new jazz album. I moved the dirt aside, placed it in the hole, and covered it back up. "Machiko, this album is really great. You would love snapping to this beat. Jazz can be listened to whenever we want now. But it's not the same listening without you."

I sighed and continued, "I have news that you won't believe." Out of habit I looked around for Matsu-san and realized she would not be looking for spies anymore, if she was even still alive. "I'm meeting my birth father. Crazy, neh? I have an important decision to make. I might move to Tokyo. But if I don't, I know I am not going back to school. I don't belong there. I don't belong anywhere. Machiko, I think about you every day, and I miss you so much." I took a deep breath and whispered, "Most of all, I'm so sorry I couldn't save you. Please forgive me."

I stood, took a tissue from my bag, covered my mouth to muffle my sobs, and walked away. After a few steps, I turned back toward the dirt pile and waved. I pictured her in front of her house, smiling as she waved back. For a moment, I thought I saw her beckoning me over to her. I stood taller and squared my shoulders. I had one final stop to make.

CHAPTER THIRTY-FOUR

"Fragrant in the Morning Sun, Sakura, Sakura, Flowers in Full Bloom."

Lyrics from traditional Sakura folk song

Stop being a coward, Yuriko. Just climb over the railing, jump, and it will be finished. I had said these words to myself over and over since I had arrived at the secluded bridge two hours ago. The sky was between the light of day and dusk. The remaining sun rays reflected in the water below. The only sound I heard was when a gentle breeze rustled the cherry blossoms. Their buds had opened up a few weeks ago to reveal the art of nature's brush. I remembered my papa saying to me, "Cherry blossoms are like life itself—so beautiful, yet so fragile that they bloom for only a short time."

The cherry blossoms had always been hauntingly beautiful to me. And they would continue being beautiful when I was no longer here to enjoy them. I put my right leg up and over the railing. I lifted my left leg and brought it over as well. I looped my arms around the handrail and my feet balanced on the ledge.

For the last few months, I had gone through the motions of being a student at school during the day. Each night I was teased by a dream where I went home to see Papa. For a split second when I woke up, I would smile because my heart was filled with love and felt whole again. And every morning my mind would shatter at the realization that I no longer had a home or a papa. In those moments I also recalled that if Papa had not purchased a train ticket for one of our neighbors, he would not have been in the center of town that day. I was torn between anger at the man who needed the train ticket and pride for my papa for wanting to help him.

My thoughts turned to our family secret. Papa truly loved me and wanted me. He kept the family honor by adopting me. Papa was unlike my birth mother who gave me away and lived under the same roof with me and pretended to be someone else.

And yet, I was torn between being happy that she had given me up and feeling rejected. Was it possible to feel both so strongly?

A mejiro bird fluttered its wings as it landed on a branch. I leaned forward away from the bridge. *Should I move to Tokyo with this Nishimoto-san and his wife? Does he have any other children? Would we even get along? Why should I be able to have the luxury of growing up when so many others lost that chance a year ago?*

I caught a glimpse of one of the last cherry blossoms as it fell from the tree. How easy it would be to jump off the same bridge that Papa and I crossed to visit Mama's grave—to simply float away like that last blossom of the season. My reasons for living had been ripped away and reduced to ashes by an atomic bomb.

As I watched the cherry blossom float down the river, the ripples turned into my papa's face. I heard his voice recounting his samurai stories. "You should have pride because of your ancestry. No one can ever take that from you. Family and honor are very important. You must never forget that." I felt his kiss on my forehead, which he always gave at the end of his stories. At that moment I became aware of the tingling bumps that covered me. It was as if I were a young child again, dressed in pajamas after my bath, and had stepped out into the cooler air of our veranda for evening story time.

But, would it honor my papa if I ended my life after he took such pains to give me a good life and a good name? I wished that this war never had happened. I would like to go back to being a little girl again, when all I needed to feel safe was his embrace.

The sun was lower in the sky. I brought my right and then my left leg back onto solid ground. My heart pounded, and my face flushed. I looked at the water one last time. "Papa, I am going to make you proud of me. I will never forget you and will honor you always in my heart. You will never be replaced. Papa, I love you."

I crossed the bridge and walked the path strewn with cherry blossom petals toward the train station to meet the man I only knew as my birth father.

• • •

As I approached the platform, I spotted a tall, handsome man in a gray pinstriped western suit pacing back and forth. There was something oddly familiar about him. At that moment he looked up and approached me.

He bowed, tipped his hat, and said, "Konnichiwa, young lady."

When he removed his hat, I noticed the thick wiry hair streaked with gray at the temples. I absentmindedly pushed my wayward frizzy strands off my face. I bowed and said, "Konnichiwa." I didn't know what else to say, so I just stood there wiping my sweaty palms on my skirt. His fingers tapped the brim of his hat during the awkward silence.

Suddenly the words gushed out of me: "Why now? Why didn't you ever try to see me before? Were you not the least bit curious about your daughter?" I heard the sharp tone in my voice and could feel eyes on me from the other passengers on the platform. But I didn't care.

He remained calm and didn't answer right away. He fiddled with the collar of his shirt against his throat before he asked, "Did you enjoy your morning swims in your koi pond?"

"What kind of a question is that? Wait, how did you—?"

My heart skipped a beat. My stomach flip-flopped. *The bow and the tipping of his hat. The morning swim. The man with sad eyes.*

I moved closer to him to get a better look at his face. He smiled at me. His eyes no longer looked sad. As I gave him a quivering smile back, I heard the words of my papa echoing in my head: *"The season changes when the last cherry blossom falls."*

AFTERWORD

The Last Cherry Blossom is based on the actual circum-
stances and events in the life of my mother, Toshiko Ishikawa
Hilliker, who grew up in Hiroshima during World War II.
She was twelve years old when the bomb was dropped on
August 6, 1945.

When my daughter was in seventh grade, she wanted me
to visit her class so I could talk about her grandmother and
all of the people who were under the now-famous mushroom
cloud. When I was younger, my mother had told me about

losing her family and home in Hiroshima. But she had not given me any specific details of this event, because the memories were still too painful for her to discuss.

After my daughter's request, my mother decided she was ready to tell me what had actually happened on the most horrific day of her life. She hoped that by sharing her personal experience, students would realize that the use of nuclear weapons against any country or people, for any reason, is unacceptable.

I continue to visit that same school each spring—to tell my mother's story. I also speak at other local middle schools about what happened in Hiroshima. My mother was never comfortable discussing her memories of August 6 in public, but I am more than happy to do that for her.

Every year, the students who have heard my presentation have expressed their gratitude to my mother for sharing such a personal, traumatizing memory. Teachers began to include my presentation in their history curriculum because they felt that the lecture gave students new insight into how children lived during the war, as well as introduced them to a culture not previously known. The students learned that the Japanese children had the same fears as the children in the Allied countries had during World War II.

I was encouraged to write *The Last Cherry Blossom* when teachers inquired if I had a book to complement my discussion, one they could add to the class reading list. I wanted to write this book not just to honor my mother and her family, but also to honor all the people who suffered or died from the effects of *pika don*. I want readers to know that the victims were all someone's mother, father, brother, sister, or child.

Originally, scientists said nothing would grow again in Hiroshima soil for many years after the bomb was dropped. Yet, the cherry blossoms bloomed the following spring. The cherry blossoms endured much like the spirit of the people—like my mother—who were affected by the bombing of Hiroshima.

SELECTED BIBLIOGRAPHY

A Boy Called H: A Childhood in Wartime Japan, by Kappa Senoh

Daily Lives of Civilians in Wartime Asia, by Stewart Lone

Hiroshima Peace Memorial Museum website, www.pcf.city.hiroshima.jp/top_e.html

Japan at War: An Oral History, by Haruko Taya Cook and Theodore Failor Cook

The Last Train from Hiroshima, by Charles R. Pellegrino

Leaves from an Autumn of Emergencies, Selections from Wartime Diaries of Ordinary Japanese, by Samuel Hideo Yamashita

The Making of Modern Japan, by Marius B. Jansen

Plum Wine, by Angela Davis-Gardner

Warriors in Crossfire, by Nancy Bo Flood

A NOTE ON JAPANESE WORDS USED IN THE BOOK

In Japan, it is customary and respectful to use an honorific after a person's name. Honorifics differ depending on relationship and age, but not on marital status or gender.

Honorifics used in this book:

san   Used after the first name for a peer or family member Used after the last name when addressing an adult (as in Mr., Ms., or Mrs.)

chan   Used after the first name of a child, male or female

kun   Used after the first name of a male child in middle school

sensei   Used after the last name of a teacher

In school, teachers address their students by their last names followed by –san. For uniformity in this book, students were referred to by their first name followed by the –san honorific. Yuriko also drops the –san prefix for Sumiyo after she is married to Papa.

GLOSSARY

arigato gozaimasu: "Thank you very much"

azuki: red bean—the main ingredient in paste used as filling in Japanese sweets and pastries

Banzai!: a rallying cry used by Japanese soldiers in battle during WWII, often associated with suicide fighter pilot attacks

chitose ame: the literal translation is "thousand-year candy," candy sticks given to children during the Shichi-Go-San festival as a symbol of healthy growth and longevity

chohei pati: a celebration held for soldiers who are about to go to war

dai-dai: a small, bitter orange

dojikko: clumsy

furoshiki: the cloth or fabric used to wrap gifts or used when carrying personal items

Ganbatte, kudasai!: "Good luck!" or "You can do it!"

geisha: a traditional female Japanese entertainer who acts as a hostess; accomplished in the art of classical music, games, and conversation; dresses in traditional kimono, wears white face makeup, and an elaborate hairstyle

geta: a type of sandal worn with a kimono

gofuku: the fabric used to make kimonos

gyokusai: an honorable death by suicide during wartime to avoid capture by the enemy

hai: "yes" or "okay"

hakama: a traditional loose pleated pants worn by men

hanafuda: a traditional Japanese flower card game dating back to the ninth century

hanami: a traditional Japanese custom of flower viewing occurring each spring

hanami dango: a sweet rice dumpling served on a stick made specifically for flower viewing and is often decorated in the colors of the flowers being viewed hashioki: a chopstick rest used in Japanese place settings

hibachi: a cooking method using an open flame

hinoki: cypress tree wood

Ie: "no"

Jigoku: fiery hell

joya: the literal translation is "young lady"; a term of endearment for a young girl

juban: an undershirt worn with a kimono

kabuki: traditional Japanese theater performed by men wearing white makeup playing both male and female roles

Kanpai!: the literal translation is "Empty cup"; a traditional Japanese celebration drinking toast

kanzashi: a hair ornament used by women in traditional Japanese hairstyles

kasutera: a traditional sweet sponge cake

Kempeitai: the military secret police

kimono: a formal Japanese robe

kirinoki: a wooden stand used to display New Year's decorations

koi: ornamental fish kept in small ponds in Japanese gardens

Konnichiwa: "Good afternoon"

koseki: an official family register (family tree)

kushu da: an air raid

mejiro: a small bird native to Japan

Miko: the female Shinto shrine attendant often referred to as a Maiden or Priestess

miso: a soy bean paste used throughout Japanese cooking

mochi: the rice dough used for cakes and dumplings

mon: a family crest

monpe: women's work pants worn during WWII

neh: a word used at the end of a statement that asks the listener to affirm what's being said, similar to "You know?" or "Isn't that so?" in English

nengajo: a New Year's Day greeting card

Norakuro: the name of a dog who is the title character of a popular WWII Japanese comic book (or manga)

norimaki: a seaweed roll used in Japanese food preparation

obi: a belt used to tie a kimono

Ohayo gozaimasu: "Good morning"

omamori: a good-luck token purchased by visitors at a Shinto shrine

Ōnusa: a wooden wand used by priests in Shinto rituals (including weddings) that is decorated with white paper streamers

osekkaina: a nosy person

Oshagatsu: the New Year's celebration

oshiire: a closet often used in homes to store futon mattresses during the day

Oyasumi nasai: "Good night"

pika don: the literal translation is "flash boom"; used by Hiroshima survivors to describe the flash of light and sound produced by the atomic bomb explosion

sakaki: an evergreen tree sacred in the Shinto religion

sakura: cherry blossoms

sakura hanami: cherry blossom viewing

samisen: a three-stringed Japanese musical instrument similar to a guitar

san san kudo: the literal translation is "three three nine times"; a traditional, ritualized drinking of three cups of sake; during a wedding, both the bride and groom drink from each cup three times to bind their ceremony

Sayonara: "Good-bye"

sensei: a teacher

Shichi-Go-San: the literal translation is "Seven-Five-Three"; a festival day for three- and seven-year-old girls as well as three- and five-year-old boys held on November 15 every year to celebrate the growth and well-being of young children

shimekazari: a New Year's decoration made from straw rope usually placed on the front door of a house or building

Shintenchi: a theater in Hiroshima

shiromuku: a traditional white wedding kimono robe

Shishi-mai: the lion dance often performed at New Year's festivals

shoji: a room divider or door made from paper over a wood frame used in traditional Japanese homes

Shou-chan manga: a Japanese comic that was first written in the 1920s about a little boy named Shou and his squirrel friend that traveled the world to find adventure

Showa Era (1926–1989): the era of Japanese history during which the Showa Emperor, Hirohito, ruled Japan; the Japanese calendar often references years as the number of years into an emperor's reign—for example, the year 1944 was called "Showa 19"

soba: thin noodles used in soup; the noodles can also be served without broth and prepared hot, cold, or fried sukiyaki: a Japanese dish usually prepared and served at the dinner table in one hot pot and shared among guests

taiko: a traditional Japanese drum

tansu: a chest of drawers

tatami: a straw mat used as floor covering in Japanese homes

temizuya: a water fountain located near the entrance of a Shinto shrine used to ceremonially purify hands and mouth before entering the shrine

Tenno heika bonsai: literally translates to "Long live the Emperor"; used as a battle cry by Japanese soldiers

tokonoma: an alcove in the main room of a Japanese home where art or a floral arrangement is displayed

Ton tsu ten ton: a traditional chant used when pounding dough during the preparation of mochi

torii: a gate most commonly found at the entrance to a Shinto shrine representing the transition from a secular to sacred area

toshikoshi soba: a traditional New Year's Eve noodle dish

tsunokakushi: a traditional wedding headdress worn by the bride

yukata: a casual summer robe

zabuton: floor cushions used as seats around a traditional Japanese dinner table

Statistics about Hiroshima

- The prewar population of Hiroshima was 350,000 people
- 80,000 people died immediately or within hours of the bomb being dropped
- 140,000–150,000 people died within the next five years as a result of *pika don*
- The bomb dropped on Hiroshima had the strength of 20,000 tons of TNT
- The nuclear warheads in America, as of 2014, have the strength of 455,000 tons of TNT

All statistics above were obtained from the following resources:

"50 Facts about Nuclear Weapons Today," www.Brookings.edu (2014)

"Army Press Notes," Harry S. Truman Library, Box 4 (1945)

"Surviving the Atomic Attack on Hiroshima, 1945," *Eyewitness to History*, www.eyewitnesstohistory.com (2001)

"Using Atomic Bomb, 1945," *Atomic Heritage*, www.atomicheritage.org (2016)

ACKNOWLEDGMENTS

This novel did not bloom overnight, and without certain people it would never have seen the outside world. First and foremost, I am grateful to my mother for entrusting me with her memories of growing up in Hiroshima during the last years of WWII.

Thank you to SCBWI Carolinas. It is more than a writer/ illustrator organization with great conferences chock full of knowledgeable programs and speakers. Through the SCBWI Carolinas, I found inspiration and reassurance from so many talented people. I have and continue to form wonderful friendships; I participated in my first critique group; and I met my agent—all through SCBWI.

Which brings me to my immense gratitude for my agent, Anna Olswanger, for believing in my writing, pushing me to go beyond my comfort zone, and finding a home for my mother's story.

I am grateful for my editor, Julie Matysik, at Sky Pony, for seeing *The Last Cherry Blossom* as a novel she wished she had read growing up. I am grateful to her and to Adrienne Szpyrka for pushing me to delve deeper into the voice of the character, while allowing me to stay true to the heart of my mother's story and culture. I want to thank Katy Betz for her artistic talent in expressing the beauty that can come from ashes for the cover art.

Thank you to the Sweet Sixteens debut MG and YA authors group and all the wonderful blogs that support and promote us.

Thank you to my North Carolina family and friends, my New England family and friends, and my Tennessee family, who have all been rooting for me and have been excited for me through this entire writing journey.

Thank you to the teachers who first invited me into their classroom to share my mother's story of August 6, 1945.

A special thank you to Rosemary, who helped me in more ways than just typing for me when I was in too much pain to do so myself.

Thank you to the Hiroshima Peace Memorial Museum and the Hiroshima National Peace Memorial Hall for the Atomic Bomb Victims, for keeping the memories of the people under that famous mushroom cloud alive.

And last, but not at all the least, my husband Matt and my daughter Sara, whom I love so much—for having faith in me when all I had was a title and an idea.

ABOUT THE AUTHOR

Kathleen Burkinshaw resides in Charlotte, North Carolina. She's a wife, mom to a daughter in college (dreading the reality of being an empty nester—most of the time), and owns a dog who is a kitchen ninja. Kathleen enjoyed a career of over ten years in healthcare management, unfortunately cut short by the onset of Reflex Sympathetic Dystrophy (RSD). Writing gives her an outlet for her daily struggle with chronic pain. She has carried her mother's story her whole life and feels privileged to now share it with the world. Writing historical fiction also satisfies her obsessive love of researching anything and everything.

Kathleen wrote *The Last Cherry Blossom* based on her mother's story of growing up in Hiroshima during World War II. She was twelve years old when the bomb was dropped on August 6, 1945.